Strange Flowers

www.penguin.co.uk

Strange Flowers

Donal Ryan

doubleday
IRELAND

TRANSWORLD PUBLISHERS
Penguin Random House, One Embassy Gardens,
8 Viaduct Gardens, London SW11 7BW
www.penguin.co.uk

Transworld is part of the Penguin Random House group of companies
whose addresses can be found at global.penguinrandomhouse.com

Penguin
Random House
UK

First published in Great Britain in 2020 by Doubleday Ireland
an imprint of Transworld Publishers

A CIP catalogue record for this book
is available from the British Library.

ISBNs 9780857525222 (hb)
9781781620410 (tpb)

Typeset in 11.75/16pt Adobe Garamond Pro by Jouve (UK), Milton Keynes
Printed and bound in Great Britain by Clays Ltd, Elcograf S.p.A.

Penguin Random House is committed to a sustainable
future for our business, our readers and our planet. This book
is made from Forest Stewardship Council® certified paper.

MIX
Paper from
responsible sources
FSC® C018179

5 7 9 10 8 6 4

In memory of Sophie Christopher,
whose loss to this world is immeasurable.

GENESIS

A LL THE LIGHT left Paddy Gladney's eyes when his daughter disappeared; all the gladness went from his heart. His days had always been so full of peace. Before Moll went he pedalled round the parish in the mornings with the post, and he herded and foddered in the afternoons on the farm where he was caretaker, and he walked the fences and checked the gaps and gates, and his wife Kit kept house in their small tidy cottage and she did the books for a few local business people, and his daughter, his only child, went to school and learnt her lessons, and they knelt every night before bed for the rosary, all three of them. And they had a radio and a dresser and a yard of hens, and a green and yielding world around them in every direction: the Arra Mountains behind them and, beyond the brow of Ton Tenna, the shallow valley that dipped across to the Silvermines Mountains, which stretched away as far as the eye could see, to the ends of the earth, it seemed, on a bright day. And the main road and the village below their house at the end of the lane, and the Shannon callows, soft and lush below the village, and the river running through the callows to the lake, glinting always on the low horizon, no matter what the light.

But the world turned cold when Moll went, and what light was cast was dappled dark with shadow. She left no note behind, just made her bed and packed her few things into her mother's old leather valise and went through the door and across the yard without a sound, and she walked down the lane to the village and she took the early bus to Nenagh and the train to Dublin. She'd withdrawn what bit of money she'd had in her post-office savings account the week before. That was all they were able to find out. Frankie Welsh the bus driver said she'd seemed happy enough on the short journey in along the Esker Line. Quiet, though, like always. She'd said hello to him getting on and he'd said he thought it was going to be a fine day and she'd agreed with him and that was about it. It was only herself got on the bus in the village, Frankie said, and he'd been surprised to have to stop. He'd nearly driven past her, she was so small. The rest of the passengers that morning were the factory boys from Portroe. She'd sat at the front just behind his shoulder, well away from the factory boys, but he couldn't see her in his mirror and he didn't like to be turning around in his seat, he said, and he didn't like to be asking any-one their business. He'd wondered about the valise all right, and the early hour of her journey, but that was the kind of wondering that a busman kept to himself, the unasked questions that filled his days.

It went around the village quickly. No one really knew what to do or say. Still, Kit and Paddy were kept busy with the visitors those first few days. People climbed the lane up from the main road in twos and threes and walked the fields down from Jamestown and Bunnacree to sympathize and speculate and reassure. Kindnesses were carried from distant hills and up from the lakeshore and laid at their door; novenas were pledged and envelopes containing handwritten petitions to Christ and to various saints, with clear instructions on timing and frequency of incantation, were left on the countertop propped against bottles or crockery the way they'd be seen. NEVER KNOWN TO FAIL was printed large on the outside of one of the envelopes and Kit folded that one away into her apron and she patted it now and then to be sure it was still there.

Things were gone funny lately, people said over and over; the world was changing fast. Everything was gone to pot. All that new talk and people's hearts and heads being turned, and the way they dressed now and the terrible music. And wars going on everywhere. Vietnam and the Middle East and only up the road in the godforsaken North. Young people were being given terrible notions and the world was a fearful place. People living together and having children before they were married at all and married people roaring for divorces and birth control, whatever the hell that was, and every kind of carry-on you could think of and plenty more you couldn't. But Moll had sense. She'd turn up, as sure as God. She'd land back any day. And Paddy and Kit stayed composed through all the talk and the heavy silences, and they turned deaf ears to the things that were whispered that they weren't meant to hear, and they were grateful to their neighbours for the help.

Kit had a cousin married in Dublin and she wrote to her to ask if Moll had called to her maybe, but the letter back was full of questions and sympathy and empty of any knowledge of Moll or her whereabouts. Moll had not been seen by anyone. Or if she had, she hadn't stood out, a plain girl from the country with a brown valise and simple clothes. What could be done? Nothing, it seemed. Prayers were promised and a mass

5

was said, or at least Moll's disappearance was alluded to by Father Coyne, obliquely and embarrassedly in a short homily invoking Saints Anthony and Jude, patrons of lost things and hopeless causes, and the small drama was absorbed quickly into the village's store of small dramas, another of those things to be remembered now and then, reminisced about, sighed over. Moll Gladney and where she could have gone. God only knew.

Paddy carried on his morning rounds because there was nothing else to do but carry on. And he herded and foddered and counted the Jackmans' cattle and sheep in the afternoons and evenings, and he walked the fences of the farm and did his jobs the way he'd always done them, and he called each Friday to their home place for his envelope, and Ellen Jackman said God bless you, Paddy, the way she'd always done, but with a deeper sincerity to it now. And people made the same old small-talk as always, though there was a funny air to it in the weeks just after the disappearance, of awkwardness, and hesitation. What could anyone say but meaningless things they already knew the answer to? Things like, Any sign? Any word from Moll? It wouldn't do to be sympathizing too much, because that way Paddy might think they were thinking what it was only natural to think: that Moll Gladney was either pregnant or dead, and it was hard to know which one of those was worse.

Kit Gladney felt betrayed by Christ, but she pushed away her crossness. She needed Him now more than ever, and she needed His Blessed Mother as much if not more, and so she did her best to stay on the right side of them. She walked the lane down to the main road through the village every evening and turned for the long hill and the Church of Mary Magdalene, proud and unsheltered at the top of it, and she knelt on the cold ground below each station of the Cross and she pleaded and promised and implored, silently, her lips moving but no sound coming out, and she held her tears for the nights when she lay in bed, sleepless always until the last hour before dawn, when she'd fall to a fitful sleep, and she'd dream that she was young again, and holding a child to her breast, and the child was looking up at her through eyes filled with love.

She cursed herself for not knowing more of the world. For all she knew, this kind of thing was a regular occurrence. She'd heard stories, of course, of people going off out into the world and never being heard from again, but as a rule when you excavated a little bit deeper it would turn out that there'd been some quarrel over land or money or a house or some kind of inheritance, or that the person who'd gone and left no trace had had a bit of a want in them or a history of trouble with their nerves. Kit didn't think that Moll had a want in her, and she had no reason to believe that her nerves had been at her: she'd always talked away and bowed her head to prayer and sung along when merriness broke out and laughed at all the carry-on and loud gregarious talk of the people who called to their cottage from further up the fields on their way down to the road. And she'd always been gracious and graceful and demure, proper, unassuming, a good, good little girl.

Kit wondered if something had gone wrong with Moll at the time of her birth, if some seed of trouble had been planted then that was flowering only now. She'd had her suspicions at the time but all of her questions afterwards had been answered curtly, with a threat of crossness. No one working on

Saint Bridget's lying-in ward at the county hospital was going to tolerate being cross-examined by the wife of a labourer. She'd been a long time in her pangs at home before the midwife had cycled down from Glencrue, and shortly after she arrived she asked Paddy had he a car, and of course that time they hadn't, but Paddy said he could easily borrow one, and she'd snapped at him to go do it so, and stop standing over them with his two hands hanging. He'd gone off across the top field to the Jackmans to get a loan of their car, and the three of them had driven in as far as the county hospital, and there was a doctor and a nurse there waiting, and Kit had suffered unearthly pain, and she'd looked in the crucified Christ's baleful, knowing eyes, and found in those moments no comfort even there. And Moll's first breath had been a long time in coming, and when at last she drew it, the cry that followed it had been low and weak, apologetic almost, as though she knew the trouble she'd caused and was afraid now of making any more fuss. Now, Missus Gladney, the midwife said, as she placed the still-pink form against Kit's bared breast. There's Her Ladyship at last. Didn't she take her sweet time about it? Didn't she make us go to great rounds?

And Moll was taken from her again and Kit slipped away to darkness, and her torn perineum became infected, and she found herself lifted from the darkness, and out away from the county hospital, and standing at a garden gate, with her hand on the sun-warmed wood of the top rail of it, and she was about to push it open and walk forward onto a soft grassy path through an avenue of trees, but a breeze was whispering in the trees, a sighing voice saying softly, Go back, go back, you have to mind your baby, and she woke drenched and her wounds seared and her vision was blurred but she could make out Paddy at the far side of the small room, and his cap twisted in his hands and his face white, and her own mother with her beads gripped whitely in her hands and she was saying, God help us, here she's back to us now, oh, thanks be to God.

But she didn't know if any of that was related to this new trouble. It didn't seem believable that a girl just out of her teenage years who'd made hardly a peep since she'd left the cradle would all at once go off bold and bareheaded without there being some root cause, some reason good or bad. The neighbours and cousins who called had no help to give in that department: some of their stories of disappearances started badly and ended worse, with bodies dredged from bogs or found twined in rushes on muddy riverbanks or submerged in ditches or loughs of water. Why people saw fit to recount these things in her presence was beyond her. To help her brace herself, maybe, for the day the sergeant and the priest would roll up the boreen with dread tidings. She was only a shout from sixty and Paddy was on the far side of it, and Moll had been their mid-life miracle, their smile from God, and now she was gone, and they felt on their shoulders the terrible weight of all the things about the world they didn't know.

They took the train to Dublin once. A few weeks after Moll went missing. Paddy wanted to get the early bus from the village into Nenagh the way Moll had done so that her exact steps would be retraced but Kit said that was foolish: they'd be stranded inside at the station that evening when they got back. They'd have to be phoning people looking for lifts and you couldn't be putting people out like that. And what good would it do them to be sitting on a bus that hour of the morning with all the factory crowd gawking out of their mouths at them? They'd look well, the two of them. The butt of every whispered joke and every elbowed rib. So Paddy sighed and went out to the shed to see about getting the car started for the morning drive but, of course, it only coughed at him and wouldn't catch for love or money.

He walked down to the shop and filled a jerry-can with petrol and put it in the car, and he couldn't find a funnel so half of it slopped down the back panel below the filler cap and more of it slopped down the front of his trousers because it was dark and awkward in the shed where the car had been parked since the middle of January. And, of course, it still wouldn't start and he thought maybe the points were damp so he took them off and dried them at the fire and he spaced them correctly and wrenched them back on, but still the sulky Austin wouldn't start so he gave the fuel pump a good bang of a hammer and that got it going. He dragged the Jackmans' new compressor over to the door of the shed to pump up the tyres and he topped up the oil and he greased the bearings and he gave the windows a good wipe down and the seats a brush off. He found a spider's web that stretched from behind the rear-view mirror down as far as the gearstick and back along to the parcel shelf, and the sun that streamed in through the space where the slats were cracked lit the thin strands of it so it shone there silky in the shard of evening light, and the size of it and the intricate detail of it and the way it spanned out so perfectly from a central point made him shiver with pleasure and wonder, and it nearly broke his heart to destroy all that spider's good work with one sweep of his arm.

The day in Dublin was long and frightening. They hadn't planned it well at all. What good was it, walking streets they didn't know, trying their best to remember their path so that they'd find their way back again? It was fine up along the river from the train station and past the Four Courts: the day was bright and the inland breeze was soft and tinged with salt, and the giant, hook-beaked seagulls were a sight to watch, fighting with each other over scraps, wheeling and swooping and screeching from the river and the rooftops. But once they got to O'Connell Bridge and saw the massing crowds crossing from the riverside to the wide main street, with the Liberator himself haughty and dark above them, hiding his killing hand beneath a stony cloak, they knew they were on a fool's errand. Even if Moll was among these people, if she was somewhere here among the buses and the rushing crowds and the pigeons and the gulls and the fumes and the river stink, they'd never find her; they'd never cover all the hard ground of this alien place.

They had an address of a place Kit's cousin said in her letter that country girls sometimes went who were in trouble. Kit had been upset reading the words *in trouble*, because she knew her daughter and she knew there was no question of that, but maybe, she reasoned, her cousin had been using the term in a wider sense, and anyway, what about it, what matter now what anyone thought? They asked a doorman who stood top-hatted and grey-tailed outside the front door of the Gresham Hotel how best to get to Granby Row, and he made a big show of telling them in a booming voice and a thick Dublin accent, his white gloves describing arcs and angles in the air so that it was hard to follow his directions because he was so enjoyable to listen to. They held hands as they passed the Ambassador

Cinema and the Garden of Remembrance and turned left and then right onto Granby Row and a line of narrow grey townhouses, their windows blinded and shadowed, and they found the one from Kit's cousin's letter and it looked the same as all the rest. Paddy drew the ring of the knocker back and let it fall heavy against the strike plate, and the booming loudness of the sound of it made him step back a bit in fright. A woman came to the door and she had a kind face and she was about the same age as Kit and the same go as her, and she had a country accent though not of their part of the country, and she didn't take the photograph from Kit's hand but put her hand behind Kit's and held it there as she looked before shaking her head slowly, saying, no, she hadn't seen that girl, but if they left a telephone number or a postal address she would make it her business to keep an eye out and to let them know straight away if she ever came across Moll Gladney from Tipperary, and she wished them every blessing God could give.

The second part of their poor plan was to go to some central place and canvass passers-by. Neither could imagine how they'd start, how they'd ever bring themselves to walk bold up to strangers to ask had they met a girl called Moll Gladney, who was twenty, with brown hair and blue eyes, and here was a photo of her, and that was a year ago and her hair was a little bit longer now. But they girded themselves all the same, and they traced their steps back from Granby Row and they stood inside the mighty columns of the General Post Office, and they asked people to look at their photograph, the one Paddy had taken with the Box Brownie the previous summer at the front of the cottage and the wall newly whitewashed behind her and her hair back from her face and the sun lighting her and her white dress. They were timid at first and disinclined to approach people: everyone seemed to be hurrying and to know exactly where they were going and what they were doing, and everyone seemed to be stylishly dressed and to be carrying briefcases and handbags and umbrellas, even though there was no threat of rain.

But after a while they grew bolder and felt able to step out from the great storeyed eave of the GPO and to ask the people who stopped to talk to them had they seen the girl in the picture, and some people paused for a few heartbeats, and narrowed their eyes, and raised the photograph closer to their faces, and Kit and Paddy's hearts would lift in momentary hope, but always the photograph was handed back with a shake of the head, or an apology, or a word or a look of sympathy, before the person rushed off again about their business. And a tall man in denim jeans and a leather jacket and round eye-glasses, like two purple mirrors, and a funny high-pitched voice took a real interest in their story, and he asked all about Moll, and Paddy wasn't happy with the way the man grinned down at Moll's picture and laughed at certain parts of their story, and the man said to them that they should take the fifty-three bus to the port and ask around out there, the security guards and the ticket people and you never know, and they thanked him and they said they would, that they were very grateful for his time and for his good advice. But, really, they hadn't the heart for it, or the courage, and so they followed the green river back to the station and they waited on a bench beneath a monstrous clock that hung on chains from the vaulted ceiling until it was time to board the train for home.

Paddy wasn't the better for the trip to Dublin. For the first time in his life he took to his bed. Or, rather, he refused to get out of it. There was nothing Kit could do or say to get him onto his feet. It was such a strange thing – stranger even than Moll's absence, because at least an absence is an invisible thing, a thing that can't be touched, and therefore pristine and incorruptible, holy almost – to see a man, especially a man the size of Paddy, inside in a bed with the late-morning sun shining in the window on top of him, with the undelivered post waiting below in the village and the cattle and sheep wondering to know where was their guardian, and all sorts of small jobs in the house and the yard and the Jackmans' barn undone. Kit tied her scarf tight below her chin and walked to the post office to let them know Paddy was indisposed and that he'd be down the next day for certain, and Bride Maher said that was fine, that was absolutely fine, they managed away grand the day of the Dublin trip, and they'd manage away grand again for another day, and he probably caught some kind of a thing that was going around up there, did he? All those strangers' hands and mouths. All those crowds of people. And no trace of Moll among them, no? No, Kit said, and she pulled the door hard behind her so the glass of it shook and the bell hopped wildly.

She walked the lane fast back up to the house where Paddy lay, and she went in through the half-door, and she closed it and bolted it high and low behind her, and she had a good look out of the back window to be sure there was no neighbour trotting down from uphill, and she checked the front window to be doubly sure there was no neighbour trotting up from downhill, and she went into the bedroom, and for the first time in her married life she raised her voice in anger, and she raised it as high as she was able. GET UP OUT OF IT, GET UP

14

OUT OF IT IN THE NAME OF GOD, I WON'T HAVE IT, I WON'T HAVE IT, I WON'T HAVE A SHOW MADE OF ME LIKE THIS, STOP THIS FOOLISHNESS THIS MINUTE. And Paddy Gladney swung around from the wall in fright, and propped himself up on one elbow, and his eyes were wide and his mouth was open, and he swung first one foot out onto the cold floor and then the other, and he stood and straightened himself, and he looked at his red-faced wife standing with her shoulders hunched and her teeth gritted and her chin jutted forward, like a man about to fight, and he hardly dared stretch his limbs or scratch himself until she turned slowly on her heel away from him and left the room. And Paddy was shocked at and grateful for his wife's anger, for the strange unfamiliar sound of her shouted words, and he was glad they had that now between them, that knowing of the limits of his acted grief, her tolerance for foolishness, and Paddy resolved that it would be the last time she'd have to strain herself that way on his account.

The Jackmans took four rows of cut turf in Annaholty bog that first summer without Moll and they asked Paddy to foot it and stack it and draw it, and in return he could keep for himself one full row of the four they'd reserved. Paddy said that he would, that he'd be more than happy to do so: it was years and years since he'd done such work, and bog air was a known restorative. And so every morning once he had his rounds done and his bicycle put away, he drove down the mill road and over past Grallagh to Kilcolman and out onto the Limerick Road and he turned off at Kilmastulla and onto the bog road, where he'd park in a wide gateway to an empty meadow and walk the last mile or so down to the soft peaty beds, the ancient blackened earth of the bog, and he marvelled at the straightness of the drills of sods, the cleanness of their cuts.

He opened a small hole in the spongy ground with his gloved hand at the start of each day's work to bury his lunch in the coolness, the way his milk wouldn't turn in the sun or his bread harden in the dry air, and he bent to his labour, lifting the moist sods out and up into small crossed stacks, tidy little weaves, so that the air could circulate in around them and dry them. And there were others in the bog that midsummer fortnight, but the plots were spaced well apart, and so he'd wave across the flat ground on arrival each day, and again as he was leaving, and the other people always waved back, because no one footed turf non-stop: a back bent to turf-footing had to be straightened every few minutes, and that straightening allowed the taking in of a good lungful of sweet air rich with minerals, and a look around at fellow toilers and up at Slieve Felim and the summit of Keeper peeping from behind it, and across the hidden river to the Clare Hills and the Arra Mountains on the near bank. And it pleased him to think that Kit was there, a few miles to his east as the crow flew, on the far side of those mountains, baking probably, or feeding the hens, or working bent-backed and bespectacled at the ledgers and the cashbooks from the shop, a tight ball of concentration. And it pleased him more to know that there was a chance, there was always a chance that Moll would be home before him. And some small bit of the gladness that had left his heart came creeping back.

Then there was a last cut of silage and two cuts of hay done, and by the time that work was finished, the turf was dried and it was ready to be bagged and drawn by tractor and trailer. The

Jackmans' only boy, Andrew, was sent with Paddy for the bagging and the filling of the trailer. Paddy had always thought he was a nice boy and a good little hurler but he was a bit cheeky at times lately, he noticed, a bit of a swaggerer. He'd told Paddy to go and find it himself when he'd knocked the previous week looking for the roll of wire that had been bought for the top fence of the haggard. And Paddy wasn't keen on the amount of spitting the boy did, or the length of his hair, or the way he kept jumping into the cab of the tractor and shifting it roughly into gear and moving up the row too fast and too far so that Paddy was left a good few paces behind, dragging fertilizer bags of turf, one per hand. It was unnecessarily wearing on his arms and legs, not to mind a bit too forward of the lad to be getting in and driving the tractor without permission, as tall as he was and well-developed for his age.

So he called out to the young lad to stop acting the maggot and to stay away from the tractor, and not to do anything unless he was told to do it. The lad was standing on the bed of the trailer by now and was looking down at him, and Paddy felt sorry for his sharp shouted words because a look of hurt crossed the boy's face, but that was soon supplanted by a dark shadow of anger. The lad jumped down off the tailgate and walked over to where Paddy stood, and came right up close to him, slowly, and said, Fuck off, Paddy, and Paddy's mouth went dry with the shock of it, and the boy's teeth were bared in anger and his eyes were flashing dark with temper, and the sound and the smell and the tongue-lolling, sharp-fanged mouth of a young collie pup occurred to Paddy, and he understood in that moment what it was to be a herded animal, to be barked at and rounded on, to be sheepish, to be cowed. The changeling boy was talking again, and his face was still up close to Paddy's, and one of the men Paddy had gotten familiar with through their silent language of nods and waves and knowing looks that fine midsummer was standing straight in the distance, arching his back forward to stretch it out. Paddy envied that man his aloneness in that moment, his command of the emptiness around him, his small dominion, because the boy in front of him, the long-haired, pock-faced adolescent he'd known since babyhood, was saying, You're a servant, Paddy, that's all you are, you're not much more than a beggar man, and my mother and father could fuck you off our land any time they wanted, and I'll drive my tractor as far as I want whenever I want. And he spat on the ground beside Paddy's foot, and he turned and he grabbed a filled bag and he hefted it and threw it so that it landed untidily on the trailer bed, and he stopped and half turned and said: No wonder Moll fucked off and left you. And Paddy stood silent and still until his heart quietened down and the silver dancing starbursts cleared from his vision, and he felt on his pained back the hint of a chill in the breeze that swept in from the distant ocean and down across the Mother Mountain to the bog.

The boy sat bold and proud on the inside wheel arch as they drove the slow roads home, gripping the grab handle lightly and singing some kind of a song, the same words over and over. He had no singing voice and the song wasn't one Paddy knew the air of, and his reedy voice grated above the tractor's oily roar, but Paddy kept his powder dry: he was shocked wordless at the boy's sudden spite and he was afraid now; for the first time in his life he was afraid of another human being. He felt shrunken to tininess, and he saw in the future a day when the reins of the Jackmans' sprawling stead were handed over to this growling pup and he was cast out, and Kit was cast out, and their cottage was levelled and the stones of its foundations pulled from the ground one by one, and the earth where it had stood rolled smooth and seeded to greenness, and grazed by careless beasts and walked upon by people who'd never know they'd ever lived. He saw Moll, standing at the top of the lane, returned to a home that was gone, wondering was she even in the right place, and he saw her walking back down to the main road, and leaving again, for all of eternity.

Paddy Gladney felt every day of his sixty-one years and he felt more than that: he felt ancient and ruined and spiritless and dead, as though there was no meaning to him or his life, as though he was a thin fleshy bag of old bones and gristle and muscles that worked from their own memory of working and not from any agency of his; that it mattered not one bit to the world or to any being in it if he lived or died; that there were dozens, hundreds, thousands, millions of creatures that could pedal a bicycle and hand envelopes to people or push them through letterboxes, and walk the land morning and evening, and count and fodder dry stock and mend a fence here and there, and what use was he if not as a father, and how could he call himself a father and his only begotten child gone from him, away from him, and not a sign of her anywhere, lost to him, lost, lost, lost?

Time is relentless, though, and heartless, and it insists on its own propagation, its own terrible replication of itself, moment after moment after moment. And just as relentless are the things that fill it, the bits and pieces that all put together add up to existence, to a life, all the big things that take up the greater part of the mind, and all the small things that sit waiting in the back of the mind, things that can't be ignored or left undone: letters and parcels and lambs and calves and fences and posts and chickens and hedgerows and Mass and confession and missing daughters and angry little sons and heirs of landed people and what have you, and cold shadowed corners of the graveyard in Youghalarra and the mulch-rich soil there, blackening and thickening with the years and the fallen leaves, biding its time, waiting to be turned, to be opened, to receive.

In the years that followed their dear Moll's departure on the Nenagh bus and the Dublin train, Paddy and Kit Gladney lived a solemn half-life of work and prayers and weakening hope, and the earth spun and the moon phased and the rain fell and the sun shone and their hearts grew heavier and heavier with grief. And a full five years went past, and more, and one Friday in spring when there was a cool breeze blowing uphill from the lake and the sun was high and white in the sky and Paddy Gladney was cleaning his boots on the scraper by the half-door, he heard the clang of the gate opening at the top of the lane, and he turned and looked, and he saw his daughter there across the yard, closing the gate behind her, like a good girl, the way she'd always been told to, and he closed his eyes and he opened them again on the greening hedgerow along the edge of the lane, and the briars and the bursting buds all along it, and the new lambs small and white in the haggard, and the strutting cockerel and the angry clucking hens, and the mucky path that ran from the half-door where he stood to the gate at the top of the lane where his daughter stood, looking back at him, smiling shyly at him like a child.

JUDGES

K IT WAS AFRAID at first that it was an apparition, not Moll in the flesh but her ghost. She extended her hand slowly towards the familiar face, and she felt heat in Moll's cheeks and the wetness of her tears, and when she drew her hands back to her own face she could taste the sharp saltiness of her daughter's tears from her fingers, and she saw that her daughter had lines now that extended from the sides of her eyes, and that her cheekbones pressed outwards against her skin. Like Thomas doubting the truth of the risen Christ, she took Moll's hands again and looked at them, turning them over as though to inspect her stigmata, the marks of her suffering, and finding none she placed the precious living's hands in her husband's hands, and daughter and father held each other's hands and none of them spoke a word in those first moments, and Paddy's cry from moments before seemed still to echo from the gable of the barn and down the gentle slopes of the hillside to the village and back up the hill again, Kit, Kit, come out, come out here, she's back, she's back, she's back. And what useful thing besides that could be said in that moment? She was back, and she was whole, it seemed, and the world was warm again and filled with life and light.

They were reverent in those first minutes and hours, filled with supernatural awe at this miracle, not quite believing yet that she was real. They laid food before her, and water and milk and brandy and tea, because what did girls drink who'd been missing for half a decade? Who could know? And they sat either side of her and looked at her as she ate, and they noticed the hardened angles of her jaw, the marks on her ears of piercings, the thickness and the length of her hair, the wave in it that hadn't been there before, the muted shade of the dress she wore and the shortness of it, so that her lap as she sat was almost fully bared. And the ring on her left hand, not on her ring finger but on the one beside it, the middle finger, a gold ring with two small moulded hands cradling a golden heart as the centrepiece. They both were crying steadily and wiping their tears absent-mindedly away, and questions presented themselves to the front of their minds in ragged jostling queues and were turned one by one away before they could be voiced; no question was enough of a question, and no answer could change the truth of the moment, that this girl was at their table, and not drowned, or murdered, or kept prisoner somewhere, but sitting here eating, prettily and silently, and her story could be told or could be kept inside her: either way they'd live.

Paddy wanted to climb the bell-tower and out through it onto the spire of the Church of Mary Magdalene and up to the summiting cross and hang from it and holler to the village and the valley and the hills and the rivers and the lake that she was home, she was back, she was safe, and every tear could be wiped away. But halfway down the lane he checked himself. There were sorrows in the village that could never be so quickly and so wholly healed. In the five years since Moll had gone there had been many additions to the roll of heartbreak in the townlands of the parish, some from the swiping blade of time, its terrible but expected cull, and some from less natural things: two fine young lads had done away with themselves not a month apart and no clue left behind them as to why; a baby had been lost soon after its birth; a man with young children had been crushed by a bullock in a pen and hadn't the use of himself any more, nor ever would again. Paddy couldn't be crowing up and down the roads about his happiness. He wouldn't be thanked for it. And so he stopped at the middle gate, the halfway point where the lane bent with the fall of the hill, and sat for a few quiet minutes on the step of the stile in the shade of the oak, and listened to the rustling meadow and the cocking thrills of wrens and sparrows, and the happy new-born bleats of lambs, and a cow's terrible lowed mourning for her slaughtered calf, and thought about how best to break his news. And the upshot of his contemplation was that there was no way to know how to do it properly, how to mitigate the hurt and offence his reversed fortunes might cause to others, and so he turned and faced into the westering sun, back up the lane to home, where he found his daughter sleeping and his wife on her knees beside her bed, her head bowed and her fingers laced together in silent prayer.

Moll had gotten the bus out from Nenagh and the driver hadn't known her because he was new, a townie lad, pleasant enough but too narrow-arsed to properly fill the dent Frankie Welsh had left on his retirement in the cracked vinyl of the driver's seat. But she'd been spotted by a few of the Ballymoylan crowd, who'd half known her to see her, and some of them had mentioned in Gleeson's shop at the bottom of Ballymoylan Hill, and more had mentioned in the Shouldices' shop at the top of Ballymoylan Hill, that they were full sure that that girl of the Gladneys from Knockagowny who went missing years ago was after getting the bus out from Nenagh and getting off at the cross below the lane up to Gladneys, and from there the whisper was carried quickly back downhill to the village, and in and out of various houses, and the presbytery and pub and shop, and for a finish a small delegation formed itself by the pump, and organized itself into an advance party of three people well known to the subjects, who would walk up the lane to the Gladney cottage and find out which or whether, and a larger body that would stand hard by the pump and wait for news. Someone then thought of the Jackmans, and the proprietary interest they had in the affairs of the Gladney family and their tiny homestead. Should a phone call be placed to their house from the post office out of courtesy before the sortie up the lane? It seemed vaguely as though that would be the correct course of action, but no one was exactly sure why. This was new territory, and how best to go about the charting of it was anyone's guess. And so, in the very same moment that Paddy Gladney rose from the stile by the gate at the bend of the lane and turned back homeward, the congregation lost its collective nerve and, with a half-hearted resolution, proposed and agreed between them all that they would wait and see, that Mass on Sunday would tell a lot, disassembled and dispersed, and no one braved it up that day to see was the prodigal daughter really returned.

So Kit and Paddy had a short time of near perfect peace, that Friday afternoon and all the next day, and the swirling questions about where Moll had been and what she'd been doing and why she hadn't written to them to let them know she was alive at least, and why she had taken herself off in the first place, were no more bothersome than a gentle breeze through the top of the half-door would be, and they were able just to look at her, to watch her sleeping, to listen to her even breaths, and the soft whistle in her exhalations that caused Kit to suspect that the girl had taken up smoking, but if she had itself what about it? And Moll slept on and on into that first night back, and the moon was huge and brilliant in the sky, and Kit and Paddy lay side by side, the soft silvery light of it draped across the blanket of their marital bed, Paddy holding Kit's hand tight, Kit whispering, over and over, Thanks be to God, thanks be to God, and they slept by unspoken agreement in short restless shifts, for fear it seemed that Moll might rise and spirit herself away again without them hearing her leaving. And when the new day dawned Moll was sleeping still, and her parents were standing by her bed, gazing at her with all the sacred wonder and unbridled love of two people beholding their cradled new-born.

She'd been in England, that whole time. She gave them the solid spine and the bare bones of her story, sitting up in bed in her nightdress, one of her old ones that Kit had kept laundered and aired with the rest of the clothes she'd left behind, because she seemed to have returned empty-handed or as good as, only a small bag on a long strap hanging thinly off her shoulder. She looked so beautiful in her laundered nightdress and so inno-cent, and there was little about her to betray the passage of half a decade of time, and she was talking softly and shyly, the way she always used to, the way that had always made Kit feel sat-isfied that she had raised a daughter who was without boldness or cheek or any impudent forwardness, and at the same time despair that she would end up a spinster, unable to put herself out there for the noticing, for the attracting of a decent man. Kit was sitting on the bed beside her holding her hand, and Paddy was sitting awkwardly further down on the same side of the bed, twisted at a funny angle so that he could see past Kit to Moll while she spoke, and neither parent interrupted the sweet song for fear it would never again be sung.

She'd worked in the dining room of a hotel, a huge place with a lobby far bigger than a church, and chandeliers like bunches of stars hanging low from a ceiling so high you could hardly see it, and she'd worked before that in a grocery shop with high narrow aisles filled with packets and jars of all kinds of strange foods, all delivered daily in lorries, and unloaded by a forklift truck, and the man who drove the forklift truck was Irish, but from Cavan, up near the border with the North, and he had a very funny way of talking, drawing out his words so that it seemed sometimes your whole tea-break would be over before he was finished with even one sentence. The man who owned the shop was from Pakistan, but he was so kind you'd nearly think he was Irish, and he knelt down on a mat to pray several times every day because he was a Muslim, and so were nearly all his customers, and so were a good share of the people in London, and there were people there of every colour and shape and size, and people who wore scarves tied up high on their heads and men who wore robes like long dresses and there were men who looked and dressed like women, and there were men with tattoos all over their arms and necks and even their faces and heads. Paddy Gladney felt, as he listened to his daughter speak, a sudden coldness, and a crawling on his skin, and a prickling in his fingertips and toes as his heart palpitated at the thought of the dangers his only daughter had faced, walking alone in a huge city, in a foreign place, surrounded on all sides by people who couldn't be known, or trusted not to rob her, or slash her throat, or defile her, or to throw her bodily over the rail of a bridge into some filthy river.

They let her talk and talk away, and she got up from bed and dressed herself in her old clothes and she appeared out to the kitchen and took her old seat at the hearth, and the sight of her sitting there where she had always sat, in the light of the open fire in the jeans and blouse that Kit had bought for her inside in Gough, O'Keeffe and Naughton's in Nenagh the Christmas before she left, hanging perhaps a little looser on her now but still fitting well, caused Kit Gladney almost unconsciously to place her hand across her chest and gently pound her heart in thanksgiving. It was true that Moll had taken up smoking, and they passed no remark on this, but Kit saw how shyly she took the box from her small, worn handbag the first time, and how her hand shook as she struck her match, how she regarded them side-eyed as she puffed her filtered cigarette ablaze, and how she grew in boldness as that first full day wore on, so that the smoking of cigarettes revealed itself to be a practised thing with her, second nature. And Kit saw how Paddy smoked with her though he'd never really been a smoker, just to put her at her ease, lovely, foolish Paddy, always doing his damnedest to ease the way of others. Kit watched and listened as Moll told story after story about the different people she'd met and worked alongside and served in the grocery shop and the hotel, and the digs she'd stayed in run by a cousin of the forklift driver from Cavan. Kit watched Moll's eyes, lit by

29

the flames that licked the bake pot in the open fire, as she sat in her old place on the hearth seat, with Paddy across from her on the far hearth seat. Kit saw how Moll's eyes searched Paddy's face for approval as she told each story, and none of the stories telling anything or revealing anything, really, about why she had left in the first place, and how in the name of all that's good and holy she could put her poor parents through five long years of living death, and flounce back in that door smoking fags and spouting stupid stories about Pakistanis and chandeliers and forklift drivers from Cavan, and not have the common decency to explain herself, to ask forgiveness, to fall down on her knees before them in contrition. But Kit pushed that crossness away and down and out from herself, and she kneaded her dough, and she tended the lamb joint in the bake pot, and she watched the happy faces of her daughter and her husband, and she broke no happy silence and she let herself be ignorant for the time being to all the whys and wherefores, and she let herself be suffused at last, purely and silently, with contentment and joy.

The peace was broken on the morning of the second full day, Moll's first Sunday back, and the purity of their joy was smirched, but that was to be expected. The world would always find its way in. Two hours before Mass, just as Paddy was sitting down to a cup of tea after his rounds of the land, Jossie Horse appeared at the open half-door. He'd walked right up the lane and had opened and closed the gate and crossed over the yard as far as the half-door without them hearing him, without causing the dog even to stir, and stood there saying nothing, just looking in through his ignorant bulbous eyes, for a joke *mar dhea*, just for the fun of it, until Kit turned around from the dresser across from the door and screeched so loud in fright at the sight of the long fecker that Moll hopped from the hearth seat, where she'd been drying her hair against the fire, and Paddy spat a mouthful of his tea back into his cup. And wasn't that a terrible shame, that a lowly person like Jossie Horse, descended from thieves, the blood in his veins tainted all sorts of ways, was the first from the parish to lay eyes on Moll, or at least the first to know for certain it was her, that she wasn't dead, and was back among civilized people, unscathed and, please God, unsullied? Of all the people.

Jossie Horse had some kind of an old story, once he'd finished his long braying laughs at the fright he'd given them all, some kind of a pretext for his creeping visitation, about a bearing being gone on the axle of his horsebox and could Paddy call down to Labasheeda when he had time and see to it for him. But Kit knew, and the knowledge burnt inside her, that he was there for a look, for a nosy, and maybe it was apt that the longest, crookedest nose in the parish was the first to be pushed in through the door, sniffing for news.

Kit had imagined Moll's return daily, and her imaginings had taken all sorts of shapes and hues and sounds: the Jackmans processing down from the big house with their best clothes on and their children strung in a line behind them arranged in descending order of size, each one holding a wrapped joint so that the sum of the carried parts was a slaughtered calf; Mary the Shop and her husband and the head postmaster from town parading solemnly up from the village, and all of Paddy's colleague postmen, resplendent in their official suits, slowly pedalling gleaming bicycles unburdened with cargo behind the brass in a sparkling honour guard of welcome; the whole of the village and every townland from the far side of the Arra Mountains to the lake's long shore, man, woman, child and beast, converging in a tightening ring on the cottage, led by Father Coyne in his shining vestments, chanting and singing and offering up praise and incantations for joy at the maiden's return. And always she felt foolish at her fantasies. And weren't her feelings of foolishness fully vindicated now? The reality of Moll's welcome-back committee was Jossie Horse, leering in the top of the door, lying about ball bearings.

He was let in but was given no welcome. He was left with his hands hanging and was allowed only a promise from Paddy that he'd drop in to him the next morning at the end of his rounds, and he was asked if he had a bearing to replace the lost one, and he said that he had, and all the while his monstrous eyes were on Moll, and Moll had her eyes cast shyly down, and was scrunching nervously at her hair, and it was as though no time had passed at all, as though nothing had ever happened, so like her old self was she in that moment, in aspect and mannerism and in the angle she held her head at. Jossie Horse was shifting his weight now from foot to foot, and Paddy was standing between Jossie and the open fire where Moll sat, and Jossie had to lean out past Paddy to regain his full view of her, and he said, Hello there, Moll, it's good to see you back. From your travels. We were all praying for your safe return, so we were. The whole place is over the moon to hear you're home with us again. And Moll acknowledged him graciously and thanked him for his prayers and good wishes, and he turned to Paddy and then to Kit, and there was a glint of reproach in his eyes, of hurt pride and offence taken, and he said, Well, I better be off, so. And he laid a little too much emphasis on *so*, the way no mistake could be made about his feelings. And he turned back towards them before breaching the doorway and said, There's no point in walking back home now because I'd have to turn back and hit for Mass as soon as I got there, so I'll hit down the lane for the village, I suppose, and see can I put down what's left of the morning there. And he cast an eye, where sadness now had joined reproach, at the wisping teapot in its cosy on the table, and the rashers laid across the pan atop the stove, and he gathered up his wounded shoulders in a hunch, and he pushed his long-fingered hands into his insalubrious pockets, and he left, and Paddy thought he heard the sound of him hawking and spitting as he clanked the yard gate shut.

Moll announced then that she didn't want to go to Mass. Kit looked at Paddy from the stove and Paddy looked back at Kit from the half-door. No words were spoken in reply. What answer could be given to such a proclamation? Kit looked up at the Sacred Heart and searched His sweet tormented face for answers, and found none there. Paddy held the fingers of his left hand tight with the fingers of his right hand and rolled the ball of his thumb over and back across the flat black stone of his wedding ring, and he looked uphill through the back window at the meadows and trees and the tops of the twin mounds of Slieve Felim and Keeper Hill in the far distance, and was surprised to notice a dusting of snow on Keeper's peak, and he thought to himself that heavy cloud must have drawn down from the north overnight and cleared away again with the dawn because the sky was a clear and brilliant blue, and Lord

God, how would they face into the church without Moll, now that Jossie Horse would have the whole place told that it was true, that Moll Gladney was definitely back?

But they held their fire with Moll and they let her return to her room and her bed without any quarrel, and they braved it up to the Church of Mary Magdalene. They took their time going down the lane to be sure they'd be at the tail end of the procession up the long hill, and they eased themselves past the backstanders and the yardboys around the door of the church, pretending not to notice anyone in particular, nodding curtly in ambiguous directions so that no one could say for sure that they'd been roundly ignored, and they slid gently into their usual seats in the second pew from the back, beneath the seventh station of the Cross, where the carved Christ, fallen for the second time on the Via Dolorosa, seemed to Paddy to be eyeing him balefully, saying, Look, Paddy, look what I suffered for you, you sinner, and here you are as bold as brass without your daughter, whom I sent back safely to you, whom I lifted gently from a dark and godless place and carried across the sea, and here am I, fallen on the ground beneath this cross to which I will be nailed, and no one to help me to my feet, and my friend Simon taken by the Romans for helping me, and as sure as My Father I'll sort you out, Paddy Gladney, I'll soon soften your cough, I'll pay you back for this, Pad, you just watch. Leaving your daughter to sleep in her bed with no Mass got. You're as bad as that Judas bollix the way you're after turning on me. And Kit had her hand on Paddy's arm suddenly, and she was squeezing his arm, and whispering softly, Paddy, Paddy, what's wrong with you? And Paddy Gladney saw a single tear drop from his cheek to the lap of his Sunday trousers, and star darkly there, like a drop of blood from a forehead pierced by thorns.

They hooked it out of the door straight after communion, and the straggling backstanders regarded them smirkingly as they shuffled back to let them past, though Kit had always maintained that to leave early, and not to wait until the final blessing had been given, was bordering on being an affront if not an actual sin. But needs must sometimes and she resolved to say an act of contrition after the rosary to make up, and to light three candles after her next devotions, and they hurried down the long hill towards the turnoff for the lane. Paddy cursed himself for not having thought to cross the road in front of the church and climb the stile into Curley's field and cross over home through the fields, because just as they reached the bottom of the long hill a motor-car drew alongside them, and Paddy could see from the side of his eye that it was a swanky, slab-sided one, and it was, of course, the Jackmans' good car, and it was being driven by Ellen Jackman, and three of her four children were in it, all the girls, ranged from late childhood to early womanhood. There was no sign of Lucas Jackman or his only son, but it was known that they went together every Sunday to one o'clock Mass inside in Nenagh because, it was said, Lucas and Father Coyne had trouble finding common ground on certain matters, and Lucas wouldn't please him to sit listening to him spouting. All four of the Jackman women were looking out of the car at the two renegades, who were standing red-faced on the roadside, and Paddy had his cap in his hand and Kit was fondling her epistle guiltily, and Ellen Jackman was saying, in quite a harsh voice, that she was going up to their house, and she was going to see this apparition for herself, and they could squeeze in if they wanted or they could follow her up the lane. There was nothing that could be said in reply because a question hadn't been asked, and Kit and Paddy well knew that there was no way to prevent Ellen Jackman from driving up a lane that her husband owned, that ran through her husband's land, that led to a cottage that was her husband's rightful property, and had been the property of her husband's father, and his father's father, and all back along into the mist, though it had been occupied by loyal and labouring Gladneys for as many generations.

Kit and Paddy hurried up the lane in silence, their hearts thumping hard. More new ground. There was a lot of it, these days, too much for their old legs to cover, for their old hearts to take. There was no way of knowing what was being said. Ellen Jackman was a kind woman but hard, with a tongue when she was cross like a bullwhip. But what offence could Moll have given her? She'd had only sympathy for them these last five years, short words but always of comfort, and she'd sent down joints of lamb and mutton and veal, and blocks of butter and cheese, and baskets full of jarred preserves she'd made herself more regularly than ever before. But, of course, Ellen Jackman would have presumed like all the rest that Moll was lost for ever; she wouldn't have nurtured that impulse to hope that Kit and Paddy had, for why would she? She had plenty of business of her own to look after, and plenty of children of her own to lavish love and worry on. Moll Gladney to her was a girl from her caretaker's cottage, from a family of high morals but low standing. So there was no accounting for her mad rush to their house now to lay her eyes on this apparition, as she'd put it, with a face of murder on her. There was no accounting for the angle she'd abandoned her swanky car at on the hard patch below the oak at the bend of the lane, or the way the middle gate was opened out as far as the ditch, as though it'd been pushed hard in a high temper, and Paddy could hear a pounding in his ears, like the steps of a giant in a cut meadow, increasing in loudness as he neared the cottage.

When they reached the yard gate they saw that the three girls were standing in a sullen ring near the chicken run, looking at the preening cock as he scratched the ground in a sulk of frustration. Paddy couldn't help but notice how womanly the eldest girl had gotten, how her summery-looking dress was blown tight to her body in the light breeze, how her hair was lifted gently from her face so that she put her hand up to keep it tidy, lifting the hem of her dress as she did so. He chastised himself, and told himself he was gone temporarily insane under the terrible and sudden weight of this series of events, as joyful as one of them was, and he checked the edge of his vision to see if Kit had seen him looking and had sensed the terrible thoughts he'd been having. Kit knew him better than he knew himself, better he supposed than God Himself knew him, and God sat at the centre of the soul of every man, looking out upon the world through that man's eyes. But Kit was a step or so ahead of him, heading for the half-door without heeding the Jackman girls at all, and Paddy saw that her epistle had been put away into her pocket and her two hands had been formed into fists, like someone about to do combat, and his heart leapt in his chest in fright. He heard a raised voice from the kitchen, and the raised voice wasn't Ellen Jackman's, it was Moll's, and the pitch and the tone and the timbre and the volume of it were so shocking and strange and yet so familiar – she hadn't made as much noise since she was a baby crying for her mother's breast in the dead of night. Ellen Jackman was standing between the half-door and the hearthstone with her back to them, and Moll was standing in the orange light of the fire, and her hair was unaccountably wet still, though she'd washed it hours before, and it was hanging lank in strands against her face, and her face was red and her eyes were blazing, and she was telling Ellen Jackman that she could fuck off and mind her own business, and that she, Moll Gladney, was no one's property, and that she was beholden to no one, and Moll shouted again at Ellen Jackman to leave her alone, to just leave her alone, and her voice was high and breaking to tears and she shouted once more, Go on now, Ellen Jackman, you go back up to your mansion and your fine husband and do your penance and I'll stay here and do mine.

And Ellen Jackman whirled on her heel and her teeth were gritted tight and her face was clouded with rage, and her eyes were flashing wet and dangerous, and she nearly knocked them as she charged out of the door, and the door flew back against its hinges and *whump*ed against the grainy whitewashed wall, and Ellen Jackman's daughters fell into step behind her and all the Jackman women marched back down the lane long-legged, arms swinging, like a company of soldiers off to war. And Paddy couldn't catch his breath. And neither could Kit. And Paddy's eyes were nearly sightless from the shock. And so were Kit's. And neither of them knew a word that could be said. And neither of them was able to lift their eyes from the floor before this dripping girl, and lay them on this changeling, this revenant, this creature that had been sent back, it seemed, from the mouth of Hell, having taken the form of their dear departed

Moll. What a trick the devil had played on them, what a terrible, evil trick! What cruelty the world contained, and the heavens, what a show they were now before God and the parish, to say they'd been so easily fooled, so easily led to believe that all their pain was gone, that they'd been smiled upon by Fate, that they'd been divinely rewarded, that their baby had been given back, when all along they had been cursed, and cursed again. Kit raised her face first, expecting in some part of herself to see that the Moll-shaped creature had turned to smoke or a pile of ash, had rejoined the flames, and Paddy looked then and he saw that, no, it was all right, it was still Moll, it was his daughter, and she was sobbing so hard that her shoulders were working up and down, and her face was contorted in some agony, in some unknowable passion, and her dear hands were held tight to the sides of her face, as though to hold the halves of herself together, and it was her, for sure, thanks be to Jesus it was her. And he knew, somehow, and so did his wife, by some perfect and unexplainable force of love, that something was wrong with their daughter, inside in her, that she was whole now but only just, and that she was in terrible, terrible trouble.

They were able, just about and by dint of dire necessity, to put to the backs of their minds, or to quash almost completely, the dark images and half-formed ideas that took shape in their imaginations when they thought about the confrontation between Moll and Ellen Jackman and the provenance of the anger that had passed between them. They had a sacred duty to set their minds and their hearts and their hands to the job of work assigned to them by God: caring for their child. Ellen Jackman had been addressed in this house in profane terms, to a wrath without precedent or any evident cause, had been cursed at by this child. They could be put out for this quite easily. They could end up walking the roads like tinkers, pitching tents of sapling boughs on common land.

The set-to he'd had with the boy of the Jackmans in the bog short years ago rang clear and true in Paddy's ears: You're a servant, Paddy, that's all you are, you're not much more than a beggar man, and my mother and father could fuck you off our land any time they wanted. And though the boy had seemed ashamed when next they'd met, and had addressed him, seemingly fondly, as Pad, the sting of the shock of his insults had never really eased; his words still smarted and cut on recollection, and Paddy had always thought of himself since as being the same go as an old crossbred dog around that boy, a ratter for the yard and barns; a creature that could be as easily mollycoddled as kicked, utterly dispensable. And this was no levelling of scores, this terrible scene that had played itself out in their kitchen, in the light of their fire: Ellen Jackman wouldn't know that Paddy had been cursed by her Andrew the same way she'd been cursed by his Moll; nor would she ever unless the screws were tightened on Paddy beyond the limits of his bearing, and he reckoned he could bear a lot; so there would have to be a reckoning, a prostration, and a giving of reparations, but not this day.

Moll was quiet now, and Kit's strong arms were around her, and they were side by side on the hearth seat, and Paddy was standing looking at them with one arm as long as the other, and all their hearts were slowing down, back to a more sedate rhythm, and the stirred dust was settling itself to a slow fall in a sudden shaft of sunlight from the high unblinded pane of the back window, and Kit was telling him to put on the water and not to be standing there staring, and Paddy knew her impatience with him, her softly dismissive voice, was feigned, a way of making things seem normal and undramatic, but still and all it worked, and he was soothed.

Paddy braved it in to the Jackmans during his rounds the next morning. They had post, but nothing bulky that couldn't be put in their metal letterbox that was bolted to the high wall outside their house. He opened the gate and he closed it behind him and he cycled in the curved driveway to the front of the house, making a mental note as he pedalled to give their lawn its first cut that week and to tend the beds he had laid the year before the way the weeds wouldn't take dominion and choke the life from the proper perennials before they had a chance to establish themselves. And he remembered then that he might not be welcome in the Jackmans' garden ever again, or on their land, or in the doorway of their house, and he felt a shaking start low in himself and he gripped his handlebars tight to steady himself, and he practised his speech of personal and proxy contrition, and he sent a short prayer heavenward for intercession, from any receptive saint, or from his mother and father, or anyone who might have an interest in these things or any hand in the doings of man and the variation of his pathetic fortunes.

Ellen Jackman was coming through her porchway dressed for town when Paddy reached the front of the house, and there was a daughter with her, the middle one it looked like, but it was hard to tell when they weren't together which was which, and Ellen Jackman told the daughter to go and wait in the car, and she turned to Paddy without a smile, but that wasn't unusual, especially when she was hurrying, and she said, Hello, Paddy, and Paddy said, Hello, Ellen, as he dismounted and proffered her post, and she told him that Deirdre had an appointment with Sherwood the dentist inside in town, and it was a pity she spent so much of her time sucking sweets and daydreaming when she should be learning her lessons and saying her prayers, and two of her back teeth rotted from her head from those blasted apple drops she was so fond of, and she'd know all about it now when Sherwood went at her with his implements, and she'd be going straight into school after her ordeal, she needn't fear. And Paddy nodded and laughed away at Ellen Jackman's story and her admonishing observations on the habits of children in this day and age, and Ellen Jackman stopped at the end of her story and she paused and said, Well. Wasn't that a shocking thing yesterday? And Paddy could only allow with a slow nod and casting groundward of his eyes that it was, shocking, shocking to the world, and he was as sorry as could be. And Ellen Jackman said, Paddy, you have not one thing to be sorry for. Moll and I will talk again, when she has her rest got. And we'll say no more about it for now. I know what it is to be lost, Paddy. Tell her to call to me whenever she wants. And Paddy Gladney felt a head-swimming mix of confusion and relief, and he felt utter love for his benefactress as she stepped gracefully across her smooth yard and into her motor-car and pulled on her leather driving gloves and glided away, and he turned his bicycle and pedalled hard after the gleaming motor-car the way he could open the gate for them and close it again behind them, with a tear of gratitude in his eye and a prayer of thanksgiving on his lips.

And so the days of the week filed on with something akin to their regular beat, and there was no further mention made of the incident, and the whole thing began to seem like something that might have happened only in their imaginations, like something you'd see happening on the television above the counter below in the pub, something that was acted out by people far away in time and space, not really real at all. And Paddy was left to do his duties unimpeded and wasn't questioned or reproached, and neighbours began arriving in the evenings, one by one at first, and then in groups of two and three, just to lay their eyes upon the returnee, to see the flesh-and-blood proof of her, and to welcome her back to the land of the living, and to ask her how had she got on, and what had she made of London, because it was known now by all and sundry where Moll Gladney had been, but still nobody knew what all the secrecy had been for, how she'd been able to put her poor parents through all that pain, though all sorts of theories swirled about, fables and yarns and tall tales and fairy stories and lascivious conjecture in some cases, darkly delicious things that could be delivered only in a whisper, from behind a shielding hand and at the point of an elbow, and met with racking guilty laughter, that filled the void where the truth would be, if they could ever get to it.

As that first full week of Moll being back came to an end, and the sun sat low in the orange sky, and Paddy Gladney finished his rounds of the fences and fields, his collie pup pricked her ears and barked beside him and spurted suddenly downhill, and he heard the middle gate clanging open as he passed from the glade below the long acre to the stand of white-flowered apple trees, and he heard the tramp on the lane of two sets of heavy feet, and as he cleared the trees and rounded the back of his own cottage, he saw Father Coyne, and Sergeant Crossley alongside him, and their faces were grave and their aspects were grim, and they were nearing the yard, and Paddy Gladney forced himself forward towards them, and he could feel a tightening in the centre of his chest, like a noose being fastened on a condemned man's neck.

He could see through the side window that Kit was at the stove and Moll was on the hearth seat sewing. Neither had stirred to see who was coming up the lane, and Paddy supposed that they were listening to the radio and hadn't heard the clanging gate latch or the tramping feet, or if they had that they supposed it was neighbours passing on their way uphill. This was, after all, the time of day when people came home from town and from their various jobs, and it would be unusual to have callers to the house so early in the evening, even in this momentous week, and everyone who might call to see the returned Moll had nearly called by now. Paddy felt himself envying his wife and daughter their obliviousness, their lack of fear in that moment, and he felt himself hoping that the priest and the sergeant would continue past the gate of his yard, that whatever cup they carried was meant for someone else's lips and not his.

But what was there to be afraid of now, in the name of God? His wife and his only child were safe, bodily at least, in the warm kitchen of their own home, and that left very few possibilities for trouble. There was the matter of Moll's slander of Ellen Jackman, but Ellen Jackman did not appear to be nursing a grudge and, anyway, she was a woman who fought her own battles and would not in a million years, Paddy knew, have seen fit to carry stories to the barracks or the presbytery. But still, any man faced in his own yard with a red-faced priest, solemn and black-suited, and a stocky high-chinned sergeant would surely feel his heart pound in his chest as his blood raced and rushed around his body. This was a scene he had envisaged daily, hourly, by the minute some days, during the missing years just ended; these officious harbingers in his yard, with the worst of news, telephoned to them by their counter-parts elsewhere, and all of them along the line only wanting to be sure they had every *t* crossed and every *i* dotted in case at all they'd be landed in hot water for failing to properly follow established procedure in this kind of a situation, and not one of them knowing or caring about the living people involved, and the new suffering ahead of them, the final extinction of their hope.

A white bloom of dog roses was quietly exploding from the thorny hedgerow by the gatepost, and a narrow rank of cow-slip and pepperwort stretched yellow and green and white among the hawthorn along the lane's edge as far as the stile by the middle gate, and all the flowers were trembling in the breeze. The priest and the sergeant turned from the lane towards the gate to the Gladneys' yard, and Paddy Gladney had a sense of something monumental and precipitous, some great shifting of the axis of his little world, so that every angle and aspect would change. But the feeling he'd had of doom and dread had lifted by some strange force of prescience: he knew, though he had no idea how he knew, that, whatever news this pair was about to break, there was no death involved; it wasn't a message about Kit's brother in America or her sister in town or about any of his scattered siblings or their progeny. Father Coyne was clearing his throat to speak, and Sergeant Crossley was lifting a tattered notebook from the pocket of his greatcoat, and there was a harp on the front of it, and there were words written in it in blue ink, slanted gracefully backwards, and they were each of them exchanging between them the greetings of the day now: Good evening to you, Paddy, Good evening to you, Father, Good evening to you, Paddy, Good evening to you, Sergeant. Are you on your own, Paddy? I'm not, no, Sergeant, Kit and Moll are inside in the kitchen. Can we have a word with you in private? You can, but would you not sooner come in to the heat of the fire? No, Paddy, this is for your ears, for now, and you can tell the women yourself in your time and in your own way.

Sergeant Crossley stood at ease and stretched his notebook-bearing arm out in front of him and read, slowly, in a clear voice, and in a more refined accent than he would use for his normal discourse, when processing through the village, say, on his leisurely beat, or conducting checks below at the crossroads for tax on cars or lights on bikes. There is a man in Nenagh, Sergeant Crossley read now, as he stood straight-backed and slant-hatted by the gatepost. And he coughed wetly and repeated his opening. There is a man in Nenagh. And Father Coyne looked at Paddy and there was a light of mirth in his kind eyes. And Sergeant Crossley was continuing, squinting slightly at his notebook as though he was having trouble reading his own handwriting, and Paddy Gladney was tipping his head forward in order to angle his ear more favourably to the portly sergeant's mouth. This man is residing currently in Grenham's guesthouse in Summerhill, and he is a stranger to this area and to all the areas hereabout adjacent and adjunct. This man aforementioned has claimed to several witnesses that he is somehow related to the Gladneys of Knockagowny, which is the townland on which we are now standing. This man aforementioned does not appear to have any business in the town of Nenagh beyond the asking of the whereabouts of Knockagowny and the house of the Gladneys of that afore-mentioned townland. And Father Coyne had his head bowed now, and his eyes closed, and Paddy Gladney's head was tilted still, and his ear was angled still towards Sergeant Crossley's mouth, and Sergeant Crossley's voice was pitched lower now, and Kit Gladney had appeared at the half-door of the cottage, but she'd made no move towards them, and Sergeant Gladney pressed bravely on. And this man aforementioned claims par-ticular connection to Mary Gladney, also known as Moll, a child of this house, recently returned from being a missing person, and this man aforementioned is an object of some sus-picion to my colleagues in the Nenagh barracks, because this man is a stranger to the area and to all areas hereabout adjacent and adjunct, and this man speaks with an English accent, and this man is black. A black man, Sergeant Crossley confirmed, and he coughed again and closed his notebook, and said, Now, and then said nothing else.

Sergeant Crossley's notebook was put away now, and the cheeks of his face were the colour of an overripe strawberry, and he was eyeing the doorway of the cottage where Moll had joined Kit, and both women were standing looking anxiously across at the three men huddled by the gate. And Father Coyne was talking, saying, You know, Paddy, there's no need at all for you to be sorry for anything, or to be protecting anyone, because you can't be held responsible for the actions of others, and I know full well the rearing your daughter was given, and the good and clean and graceful way that you and Kit have always lived, and I know better than anyone that you are faithful people, and that your consciences are clean, but sometimes Nature has an aberrant way about it, and we are all to greater or lesser extents slaves to our animal natures, and we're all burdened with the need and the duty to deny and to subjugate and to conquer these animal natures. Now, I've spoken myself to the man in question, and he was quite forthcoming, and he claims to be very seriously involved with your daughter, though he wouldn't elaborate any further on the nature of their involvement, and he claims that she's been missing from their shared accommodation in a house in Notting Hill, west London, for over a week now, and I have no reason to believe or to disbelieve anything the man says, and I'm only relaying to you now what was said to me, and the man speaks in a very mannered way, softly and gently, and does not appear in any way threatening or uncouth.

Paddy couldn't properly follow the priest's words or gauge the precise meaning or import of them, and he felt the cooling of the evening air as the sun dropped below the Arra Mountains, and the shapes of the trees and the fence posts and the hedgerow and the flowers blunted and blurred as the clear light of day softened to gloaming, and Paddy Gladney stood at his full height, and addressed his visitors, and he formed his words carefully, and he held the tremble from his voice. Thank you, Sergeant. Thank you, Father. I'll drive in to Grenham's this minute and I'll attend to this. I don't know who this man is or why he's telling such stories but I can assure you that my daughter Moll is not involved with any black man, nor was she ever, and there is no connection, high up or low down, between this man and my family. And Paddy Gladney turned to look at his small family in the doorway of the house he'd been born in, where his father had lived all of his life and his mother had lived the greater part of hers, and he wondered what would happen if he sat into his car and drove down the lane, and onto the main road, and out past Borrisokane, and on to Portumna and Loughrea and Galway, and into and through that bright city he had heard about but never seen, and kept driving and driving until the road ran out against the ocean, and he plunged himself into the waves and struck out for a distant shore.

But he caught himself and he pushed that fantasy aside, because he knew that that was the wild and fevered thinking of a man who was tired to death of the trials he'd been sent, and he wasn't that tired yet, by a long chalk. He felt a great reserve of strength still in his arms and his legs, and a steadiness in the centre of himself, even while his heart pounded hard in his chest at the thought of the task he was about to undertake. He'd been stretched out taut, racked to breaking in the years just gone, picturing his daughter dead, her resting place unmarked, her eyes plucked, her flesh sloughed, her bones scattered across a seafloor, shifting with the tides from place to place. And yet she was back, and she was whole and, yes, she was holding her secrets fast to herself, but that didn't matter, and now, it seemed, a story had arrived under its own steam from England, in the shape of a gently spoken black man from the land of the old enemy, and there was a strange feeling of rightness about this queer situation, of inevitability, of Fate's ineluctable will being done.

Paddy saw Father Coyne and Sergeant Crossley to the middle gate and he declined an invitation from Father Coyne to bring Moll to the parochial house to see him because he knew Moll wouldn't want that, and he promised to let Sergeant Crossley know if the black Englishman caused any trouble, and Sergeant Crossley offered to arrange for someone from the Nenagh barracks to call to Grenham's with him and Paddy said, No, he was sure he'd be fine, Grenham's was a small house and well-staffed and, anyway, he might take the man into the Swagman's Inn or down to O'Meara's Hotel, the way they could have their conversation in the open, privately but in the presence of others, and that surely would obviate the risk of aggravation or unpleasantness, and Sergeant Crossley agreed that that was the best plan, and just as Father Coyne opened the passenger door of Sergeant Crossley's Renault van he turned to Paddy and said, Paddy, if there is any truth to what he's saying, will you be sure and find out is he a Catholic at least? And Paddy promised that he would, though he couldn't help feeling that this request from Father Coyne was rather adding insult to injury, and he thanked both men again for their time and for their ministrations.

Paddy breathed deep of the cool clean air as he stepped back up the lane to the yard where Kit and Moll were standing wide-eyed still at the half-door. Go in, Paddy said, and his eyes were flat, expressionless, and his voice was low. They turned wordlessly for the kitchen ahead of him. Kit held fire and waited. Do you know, Paddy began, addressing his daughter, why those men, the priest of this parish and the sergeant from the barracks, were here? Do you have any idea? No, Daddy, she replied, and she took her seat at the hearth and turned her face to the flames, and there was a glint from her eyes where the light of the fire was reflected in her threatening tears. Do you not? No, Daddy. Well, I'll tell you, so I will. I'll tell you now. And Kit broke her silence at last and she shouted at her husband for the second time in their long marriage, ARRA WILL YOU GET ON WITH IT SO IN THE NAME OF GOD, and Paddy nodded, as though in concurrence with his wife's crossness, as though to emphasize the appropriateness of it, given the circumstances, and he went on, all the time looking at his daughter's face, and she looking not back at him but into the dying fire.

There's a man inside in Nenagh, a stranger known to none, going around telling anyone who'll listen that he has a connection of some sort with Mary Gladney, known as Moll, from Knockagowny. And Moll looked up at him now and her face was full of fear and she said, in a whisper, Oh, no, no. Oh, yes, Paddy said, as though in contradiction, as though Moll's anguish was a simple denial of the reality of the situation and no more. Yes, Moll. He has it all off. He even spelt it right for Benjy Crossley's notebook. Because you can be certain sure Benjy Crossley can't spell it. Moll Gladney from K-N-O-C-K-A-G-O-W-N-Y, he's looking for, or so he has half the town told directly, and the other half has been informed second hand, as has most of this parish and every other hinterland of Nenagh. Kit was sighing now, and she was holding a tea-towel to her face so that only her eyes were visible, and she was steadying herself against the edge of the kitchen table, and her eyes shone with a desolate light. And Paddy still was talking. That man inside in Nenagh is an Englishman. And here Paddy paused, and he lifted his chin, and he cleared his throat before delivering the final blow. And that man inside in Nenagh is a black man. And his wife and his daughter moaned in unison.

Alexander is his name, Moll told them in a whisper. A man of twenty-one or twenty-two. He worked in the same hotel as Moll, as a waiter. He took a terrible shine to her. He walked her home night after night, right up to the railing outside the door of her digs. To make sure she got home safe, he always said. But then he'd always linger, and when she'd make to go inside he'd always grab hold of her arm and force her to stay outside talking, and it was a very quiet street and dark, and he'd stand close to her, holding her arm, and saying things to her in an urgent voice and she didn't understand half of what he said and one night her landlady saw what was happening from the window of the front room and she sent her husband out to run him off, and he called Alexander a horrible name and threatened to beat him up, and Moll had felt sorry for him when he'd been called that name, and she'd said as much the next day in the dining room of the hotel before the service started. And that had only made things worse. He declared then that he loved her, that he wanted to marry her, that she could live with him and his family in their house in Notting Hill for which they'd been given a lifelong leasehold by a housing association and that he'd always look after her and he had all sorts of plans and promises, every time he came near her, and he continued to walk home with her, though she gave him no encouragement, but he'd stop short of the doorway out of fear of being spotted again by the landlady's husband and she'd hurry inside and that was all there was to it until she'd gathered up her few bits and taken her last week's wages and left London on a day packet for home.

Paddy said, Right, and made no further reply to his daughter's story. He left Moll sobbing and Kit shushing in the kitchen and made for the shed. The motor-car started easily enough, with only the bare amount of choking of the carburettor and pumping of the throttle, and he eased it out into the yard, and he looked at Kit and Moll at the half-door as he headed for the gate, chickens flapping panicked before him. He stopped and rolled his window down and said, Will I clear him, so? And Moll nodded and her face was white and streaked with tears, and Kit also nodded and she walked forward from the threshold to the window of the car and she put an envelope in Paddy's hand. Give him that, she said, if he lets on not to have the price of his journey home. And Paddy looked up into his wife's face and saw there, for the first time since the early days of Moll's disappearance, an expression of perfect bewilderment, and terrible fear, and terrible tiredness, a hunted look: she was an old woman.

The lane was dry and he had no trouble rolling to the middle gate and through it and down to the road, freewheeling on the down slope as was his habit in order to save fuel, and once he made the cross he turned right for the Esker Line and the town of Nenagh where a black man from England waited for him in Grenham's guesthouse and he wondered at how life could be a certain way one minute and a different way altogether the next with no effort at all from the person whose life it was. For a man to do his duty now was not enough, it seemed. To live a Christian life, observing all the obligations that entailed, doing his work and minding his wife and daughter and saying his prayers and going to Mass and the odd hurling match. Why had these chaotic things been visited on a man so inclined to peacefulness and contentment? A daughter turned unaccountably to flight and madness and this visitation from a dark stranger. It was like something out of a book, one of those affronting ones that were banned for being a danger to the morals and the mortal souls of decent people. He'd had enough of it now and he'd have no more. The black was going to be cleared and Moll was going to explain herself and her missing years and her impertinent talk of penances and mansions and she was going to apologize to Ellen Jackman and she was going to conduct herself properly in future and she was going to kneel for the rosary every night and go to Mass every Sunday and help her mother in the house and yard, and none of this was going to be spoken of again. A line was going to be drawn under it once this man was told that whatever notions he had about being engaged to a good Christian girl from a house of faithful people he could relinquish immediately, and he could turn around now and take himself back to whatever corner of the world he came from.

And Kit was left with the crying child. Like a new mother, she wasn't sure of herself. She felt a smoulder of rage being bellowed to flame inside her at this new development but she shut her eyes and she joined her hands tight together in the wide pocket of her apron and she took a deep breath and held it, and after a few long moments the flame died for want of oxygen and she was able to be reasonable, or to speak with some passing semblance of reasonableness at least. The child was hegging and sobbing still and her hair hung over her face and she was gripping the leading edge of the hearth seat at either side of herself, as though to steady herself, to keep herself upright, so tight that her knuckles were drained white of blood. Kit moved towards her, thinking all the while of the most blessed of mothers, and how the trouble would only have started for her once her Child came back from the dead. Because those Pharisees would have come calling, as sure as God. The scriptures made no mention of it but she must have lived on, back in Nazareth. They'd never have let her off with it. They'd have come calling for certain, once it got out that her Son had escaped the tomb, and they'd have made her pay.

Tell me the truth now, while your father isn't here. While the poor man is inside in Nenagh, facing down the heathen. Tell me the truth now, Moll, and shame the devil. But Moll was silent still, except for a whimper and a snuffle here and there, and Kit could feel her good temper beginning to gallop away wild again, and she had to keep a tight rein on it, she knew, she had to keep it at an easy canter, because if she lost control of it all hell would break loose. This was too much, too much by far for any person to have to contend with. And Kit felt a distant pang of longing for the life of eventless wondering and prayer and untroubled heartbreak that she and Paddy had lived for the years just gone, and she admonished herself severely for it, for the unforgivable ingratitude it would constitute to regret any single aspect of her daughter's return; she was obliged, she knew, to give thanks even for the sight and sound of Moll cursing her husband's employer and their landlady, the wife and the plenipotentiary agent of the owner of the ground on which their home stood, and implying all sorts of filthy things; and that was the devil's fault, she knew, because the devil had a great trick, ancient and well-tried, of seizing the bodies and the tongues of young women, and leading them into badness, sometimes only for moments, but a moment was

55

often enough for a soul to be cast from the path of righteous-ness and set on the road to perdition.

Kit had an idea that some truth was close to being told, something revealed about her daughter that might lead even-tually through its revelation to redemption, though redemption for what misdoings Kit could not tell. She had an idea or two about the true nature of her daughter and her time in the dark-ness, born of instinct and intuition and the inarticulable knowledge of a child that can only be possessed by the bearer of that child, by the person from whose cells the child was grown. But there was no way that Kit could think of to begin a conversation about that kind of thing, so she reached uncon-sciously for her epistle, and caught herself and put it down again, and she looked across from where she was sitting at the kitchen table to where Moll was sitting on the hearth seat, and she told Moll to put a log on the fire, and she did so, and she pushed her hair back from the side of her face as she straight-ened again, and Moll all of a sudden in tremulous but clear voice started to talk, and Kit knew just enough about the fra-gile mechanics of such moments to be fully silent, to barely breathe, as her daughter made her first confession since her teenage years.

I never felt right inside, Mam. From when I was about ten or eleven. There was something wrong with me. Something I couldn't put a name on. Miss Fahy said something one time in religion class about something that came a bit close to describ-ing what I felt, and she said that it was natural and unnatural all at once, that because we were formed from the same stuff as animals that we were beholden to our animal natures and that we should pray whenever we felt any strange urges and ask

God for strength and they would go away. But mine never went away. I was so ashamed of myself. It was this monstrous thing inside me, and it came in upon me every now and then, like the tide comes in on the sand, covering it completely and changing it, and there was never any way of stopping it or of reducing its power, and I never had a choice but to give myself to it, and I was always ashamed. I did things. And when I did it was like someone else was doing them and not really me. Just some other thing acting through me, using my body, possessing me. And then I thought maybe I was possessed, that the devil was stuck in me, and I decided to do away with myself. My plan was to get a bus to Limerick, and then to Ennis, and then to Lahinch, and I was going to walk to those big cliffs away up from Lahinch and throw myself off. But then I thought I'd be doubly damned for being a deviant and a suicide, and I made a new plan and I drew out my money from the post office and went to London on the ferry bus from Dublin port, and it was easier over there not to feel every minute as though I was damned to hellfire, and it was easy to feel as though I was dead in a way, because I thought to myself that you and Daddy would presume I was dead and so that would be the same thing anyway, and I felt terrible about that in one way because I knew how sad you'd be, but it was easier in another way not to have to feel sorry every second for the things in my head. Because there's a world of people over there, millions and millions of them. And loads of them were like me.

An animal lowed in the distance and some nocturnal creature landed on the roof of the lean-to and scratched and clattered there before flying away, and a car passed through the village downhill from them as Kit tried in vain to form all her

57

questions into one. The girl had spoken now, and still Kit knew as little as she had before she spoke. She felt again her temper rising for the third time and this time it heated fast and exploded upwards like boiling milk and she heard herself shouting and she was surprised at the loudness of herself and at the words that were coming from her mouth. What did you think, Moll, in the name of God? That you were the first person in the world to have a dark thought? How is it you hadn't a tongue in your head for twenty years and now you've said more in a few days than any woman has a right to say in a lifetime? What kind of patience do you think your father and me were given? Could you not have written a letter in all the time you were gone? I'll tell you what's wrong with you, Mary Gladney. You've too much time for yourself. You give yourself too much consideration altogether. 'Tis our own fault. Mine and your father's. We made a fool out of you, mollycoddling you, asking nothing of you, allowing you to sit there grinning and never asking you to do a hand's turn. You thought too much about yourself, so you did. Little lady of the manor, you were. You did things? You did, I'd say. Whatever they were they were the first things you ever did. I don't know what the things you did were and, God help me, God help us all, I hope I never know. Lord Jesus, your poor father. You'll be the death of him. That good man. Gone off into Nenagh to try and sort out your dirty, dirty mess. God help us all.

Kit Gladney found herself for the first time raising her hand to her child, and Moll's eyes were closed tight and her cheeks were wet with tears and the strength left Kit's arm and she lowered it to her side. Moll was here now, changed but whole. All the other parts of her daughter's story, she knew, would reveal themselves piecemeal, or could lie unobserved in the gloom of the past. And the nature of the things that Moll had done, which she felt such shame over, took solid shape in Kit's imagination for short moments and fragmented again and melted away, like the patterns of light on the insides of her eyes, when she squeezed them tight shut, that bloomed and starred and disappeared when she tried to fix her focus on them. As far as she could tell her daughter had killed no one, had stolen from no one, had harmed no one only herself. And what about it now if she had strange urges? Kit had felt the sickly sweet breath of such things herself, one time. She'd never acted on them but then again she'd never had the opportunity. She was busy minding her parents and her brother and sister until the old people died in quick succession and her silent brother married, and then her sister, to a man with a good job and a Pioneer pin, and then she got married herself and Paddy had been close to forty but he'd been full of conjugal enthusiasm and they'd made up in the light of grace for a lot of time spent longing. If Moll had sinned her sins would be forgiven. Moll had been sent a trial, had been cast into the desert to hear all the devil's invitations to treat and to deal with them. She could cleanse herself quite easily. All that was required for forgiveness was contrition, and that was evident in abundance, and there were plenty of confessionals in the country besides the one that Father Coyne rested his great bulk in every Friday afternoon and evening; Paddy and herself could easily drive the child in the road to Limerick city, or over as far as Birr or Tullamore or any of those places and they all full of dark and welcoming confessionals of carved oak where returned prodigals could bare their sorrows to gauze-blinded priests, and it was unlikely there'd be anything said to any confessor that wasn't heard before, and Moll could light a whole bank of candles after her prayers of penance, and Kit would gladly help to fund the lighting of them, and they'd carry her back with every stain and smirch removed from her precious tormented soul.

And Kit said as much to Moll, and said that she was sorry for shouting and for calling her that name, and Moll looked as though she might be getting back to herself, coming to some kind of an accommodation with herself and with her situation, and Kit went to the hearth seat to embrace her, and there wasn't a screed of embarrassment or awkwardness between them that was ever known, in spite of all the alien talk and shouted words that had passed between them, and they clung tight to each other a good long while, and they forgot momentarily all the dramas of the day and the mission that Paddy had been sent on, and all their fears and worries melted away in the warmth of the open fire and one another's arms, and after a while they heard the sound of a car on the lane, and it was Paddy's car, and they went to the door to greet him, and they saw in the passenger seat the eyes and the ears and the mouth and the white teeth and the tie-knotted neck of a man. A black man. Alexander. Kit had known in some part of herself that this would happen. That, in spite of the way he'd gone off all revs and hard business for himself, and in spite of the clear mandate he'd been given at the door of this house, and in spite of his stated intention and the envelope of banknotes he'd been equipped with, Paddy Gladney would land back from town with the black man in tow. And that he'd have some kind of a half-baked sob story as to why. And he went about starting the sob story in the moonlit yard before even getting the black man out of the car, but Kit cut him off, and said, Get him in. Get him in this instant before anyone passes up the way and sees us. And it was clear when Paddy opened the passenger door and put his hand in to help the black man to extract himself that the black man was drunk: his head was wobbling on his shoulders and there was a breeze of porter wafting from him, and he was making some kind of an attempt at talking but all that was coming from him was a low, strangled noise, and Moll was standing beside her father now looking in at the black man and she was saying, Oh, Alex, why are you drunk? You don't even drink. And the black man was looking up at her now from his reverie and his mouth had stretched and broadened into a smile of the whitest teeth that Kit had ever seen and his eyes were shining with drunkenness and love. And Kit could see that this pair were far better acquainted, and had more between them, than her daughter had let on. And Kit knew further, though she wasn't exactly sure how she knew, that this long, suited stranger was going to be a part of all their lives.

Alexander was helped inside and put sitting at the table and was given tea and a plate of ham and bread and a saucer of butter and a knife and fork. But still his head was wobbling and his eyes were full of watery light, and he was saying, Thank you, thank you, over and over again, and that was all he seemed at the time to have to say for himself. His hands were twice the size at least of Moll's, and Moll had one of them held in both of hers, and she was looking imploringly at him, and she was on the verge of getting cross, and she was saying, Alex, how on earth did you find me? And she was telling him that he shouldn't be here, he shouldn't have come.

Kit stood by the sink with one hand on the cold rim of it and one hand on her hip, and Paddy sat across from Alexander and his daughter, and he said he'd had no choice but to get Alexander away from the town and out here to safety. When he'd arrived at the door of Grenham's he was told by the lady of the house that she'd put the black man out because he'd abused her. He'd taken offence because she'd rung the barracks to inform them of his presence and had told them his business, as she'd put it, but she assured Paddy that that hadn't been the case at all, that two young guards had been in the café downstairs having a cup of tea and a sandwich earlier in the day, two of the new lads fresh from Templemore, and that they'd observed the black man with their own four eyes and they'd heard him with their own four ears asking people did they know whereabouts was Knockagowny and did anyone know a girl called Moll Gladney, and it was they radioed the Masontown barracks and it was likely Benjy Crossley who had phoned the parochial house in Youghalarra and none of it was her doing but all the same he stuck in her and addressed her as *woman* and she certainly wasn't having any of that from anyone. Out on his ear he was put.

Paddy followed a very short trail to the bar of the Swagman's Inn two doors down from Grenham's where he'd found Alexander on a high stool drinking a pint of Guinness. And a small ring of blackguards around him, laughing at him. Mickey Briars and Scaldy Collins and a few more Paddy didn't recognize, real townies. And Scaldy Collins was in his official IRA uniform, or the half of it he had left, the jumper and the black beret, and he was making out he was a real high-ranking Republican altogether, asking Alexander where was he from

62

and what his business was and what his affiliations were and was he a British soldier or a British spy and Alexander was the worse for the porter he'd been drinking, and he was laughing away thinking it was all only a great bit of sport, and Paddy had a strong sense from the first moment he laid eyes on him that there was no harm whatever in the boy, in spite of the length of him and the great size of his hands and the blackness of his skin. And he'd only been drinking porter in the first place out of pure politeness, Lar Grace the barman told Paddy, or so it seemed to Lar anyway, because of the way he was after landing in, suitcase in hand, as a refugee from Grenham's guesthouse, God help us.

And Paddy swelled a bit as he told the next part, about how he'd elbowed his way into the middle of the circle of shapers and said, Alexander, I'm Paddy Gladney, it's nice to meet you, and he'd put his hand out to Alexander and Alexander had shaken it, and Scaldy Collins had clicked his boot heels and ordered Paddy to stand down, and Paddy had rounded on Scaldy and told him to go on away to fuck out of it, to go up the fucking North if he was so eager to fight the British, besides standing around in pubs three hundred miles from any danger, in his fancy dress in the middle of a gang of go-boys spouting shite, outnumbering an innocent visitor to these shores by five to one. And Scaldy had taken fierce offence at this, and had issued all sorts of warnings to Paddy, about being a colluder and a collaborator, and what might happen to people like that, and Paddy had looked him square in the eye and told him he talked a great fight, and Mickey Briars had creased up laughing at this, and he'd agreed with Paddy, saying, It's true, Scaldy, in all fairness to Paddy that is pure true. If talk could free Ireland we'd have the six counties back long ago and you'd be crowned fucking High King!

And after a while the black man, whose name they knew now to be Alexander Elmwood, came around a bit and he ate a good share of the ham and bread and he drank a mug of tea but he snubbed the butter and Paddy thought it odd that a man would eat a sandwich dry like that but he knew enough about the world to know that darkies had different habits from whites, were composed differently, had different constitutions. And Alexander Elmwood begged their pardon several times over, though it wasn't clear for what it was being begged, his inebriation they supposed, and every time he spoke Moll shushed him and squeezed his hand to stay his words, and he rose for a finish and asked the whereabouts of their facilities, and Paddy and Kit were concomitant in their thanks to God that they'd built an indoor lavatory with a sink and mirror the year that Moll had been sent the pains of womanhood. And Alexander Elmwood stooped beneath the low lintel and shuffled long-legged and rumpled down the short hallway, and they listened to him retching and vomiting, and Kit told Moll to take him down a fresh towel, and she did, and she was gone a long while, and Kit and Paddy strained to listen to the low mutters of their conversation but they could pick up none of it, and Moll came back up the hall on her own, and she said she'd put him into her bed and she would sleep in with her mother that night and Daddy would have to sleep with Alexander, and never in his wildest imaginings did Paddy Gladney ever think that his first night sleeping without his wife alongside him since the day his daughter was born would be spent inside in a bed with a gigantic drunken black man.

But Alexander was out cold and he hardly stirred when Paddy joined him and the next morning Paddy was up with the lark and he checked before he left for his rounds of farm and roads that the stranger was still breathing, so quiet and still was he, and when he went out to the kitchen Kit was waiting with his tea and toast and she had tarts made and ready for the oven, and there wasn't much to be said between them, they'd have to go about their day as normal and see what the evening brought, and Kit kissed her husband's cheek before he left, as tenderly as she ever had, and when Paddy Gladney arrived home that early afternoon having walked the land and done his bit of foddering and his round of post up hill and down valley, he found his wife and his daughter and Alexander Elmwood at three sides of his kitchen table, and there was a chair waiting for him on the fourth side, and Kit said, Sit down, Paddy, I have something to tell you, and Moll Gladney and Alexander Elmwood looked across at one another and were silent. Kit's voice was even and measured, and had an edge of culture to it not normally present, except when speaking to Ellen Jackman or Father Coyne or to her brother's wife on the payphone in the village once or twice a year. She sounded a bit like a newsreader or a continuity announcer on Raidió Éireann. And the strange sound and the levelness of her deadpan delivery were nearly as amazing as the news she was calmly breaking.

Moll and Alexander have a son, Joshua, who is at this moment sequestered in the Coachman's Inn in Borris-in-Ossory, in the company and care of his grandparents, Barney and Delilah Elmwood. Alexander left them there yesterday when the Dublin to Limerick bus made its usual convenience stop, and he continued on alone to find his wife. Wife? Yes, Paddy. Our daughter is a married woman. This man, Alexander Elmwood, of Notting Hill, west London, is our son-in-law and the father of our grandchild.

Go on, Paddy said, and felt immediately foolish. Shouldn't he have more to say than that? But they were married at least, they had a certificate to prove it from the Royal Borough of Kensington and Chelsea, London, and Kit pushed a letter across the table towards him, and Moll handed him his reading glasses, and the letter was written in blue ink and it was from a priest explaining, in a curt, backwards-tending cursive, that he had married this couple, she a Roman Catholic and he a Pentecostalist, in the church of Saint Francis of Assisi in Notting Hill on the first day of July 1977, and both parties had sworn to raise children of their union in the Catholic faith. Paddy Gladney reddened at the thought of it. His daughter fat with sin at the altar of an English church. Who was there? he asked. At the wedding? Only the priest and Barney and Delilah, the girl said. And a sacristan from Mayo and an organist who was nearly blind. Small mercies, Paddy said. And he recovered himself a little. Maybe he was wronging her. He didn't want to think too much about times and what might have happened in what order. And, anyway, she was a married woman now and beyond reproach. He whistled softly. A blind organist! By God. That's a fair one. His daughter pressed her advantage. Yes, Daddy. She had a white stick and everything. She came that day especially. She came as a favour to the priest. By God, her father said again. That is a good one.

Still Alexander was silent, looking steadily at the table-top, but Paddy could see that he was smiling, and there was

66

something childish and genuine in the boy's smile. Something that would cause you to trust him out of hand. But Paddy knew the danger trust could lead you into. How ill-advised it was to believe your waters when smooth would run so for ever, and not rush and break to torrents.

Kit went on in the same placid and heightened tone: Joshua, our grandchild, is just shy of a year old. Mr and Mrs Elmwood have travelled to Ireland with their son and their grandson, to see could they reunite child with mother, and husband with wife, so that the natural order of things might be restored.

And the story made perfect sense to Paddy and made no sense at all. By God, he said again. And he rose from the table and went out of the door and no one called him back. And he strode the fields across the hill to the Jackmans and he passed in along the narrow yard through their farm buildings and their empty stables to the back door of their house. He met Lucas near the haggard gate and he asked could he be absolved of his evening rounds of the land. And it occurred to him then to ask further could he borrow Lucas's motor-car. It would make a better impression on the foreigners. They might be more inclined to relinquish custody of the child to people driving a big, expensive car. He told Lucas that he had to drive as far as Borris-in-Ossory on unexpected business and he wasn't convinced the Austin wouldn't leave him on the side of the road because it was prone to a bit of heating up lately and the head gasket was surely going to blow. Lucas looked at him for a long moment, a mixture of worry and quiet surprise on his face, before saying that he could, that he'd walk the land himself for a change, and that Paddy was welcome to borrow the car once he left him the keys to his Austin just in case he had to go anywhere in a hurry himself. And Paddy sat into an automatic car with leather seats for the first time in his life and he guessed that the D on the strip beside the gearstick stood for Drive, and he eased out along the Jackmans' curved driveway and he saw Lucas in the rear-view mirror standing watching him leave with a funny expression on his face, and he wondered what the letters BMW stood for on the steering wheel, and he decided he didn't care, and he drove down the Well Road to the main road and over to the lane and back up to his own house, and he swung into the yard in that gleaming, burbling rich man's car and he told his wife and his daughter and his son-in-law to get themselves ready quickly before the day was gone: they were going to Borris-in-Ossory to meet Joshua Elmwood.

The boy was white. They couldn't understand it. He had black hair, true enough, and fullish lips, and his eyes were brown, but his skin was milky white. How was he so white? It happens sometimes, Barney Elmwood said, and he sounded like a man who was singing: his words went up and down and were drawn out to the last, and his voice was gravelly and deep at the ends of his sentences and high and sweet at the start of them, or the other way around sometimes, and his navy suit was a little crumpled but was cut sharply and his shirt was brilliant white and his shoes shone like the sun and he wore a hat with a feather on the side of it and his hair and his moustache were grey and there were lines of age at the sides of his eyes but they sparkled with mischief, and his step was light and youthful. They were standing in a semi-circle at a fountain in the green area at the centre of the hotel grounds around Moll, who was sitting on a bench before the fountain with her son on her lap, his eyes closed and his arms clasped tight around her neck. I have seen it before, Barney Elmwood said. I sure have. Sometimes when there's mixing it goes fully the daddy's way, and sometimes it goes a little both ways, and sometimes it goes fully the momma's way. I have seen stranger things. I have seen two black parents with a baby ghostly white. I have seen white parents with black babies. And Paddy and Kit were half hypnotized by the sound of him, and he was telling them how you could see Alexander in Joshua's eyes, and you could sense Alexander's spirit mixed up with the boy's spirit, and skin was only there to make a body waterproof, and the colour of it mattered not.

And Barney Elmwood's wife Delilah spoke then, and Kit was amazed that a voice so soft and demure could come from a set of lips so massive, from a body of such astonishing girth, and she said, This is true, what my husband says, this is God's truth and the truth of righteous people, but also there is this truth: a black family in Notting Hill cannot raise a white boy, it will be too hard for him, he will not be accepted. He needs to be here with his mama. Isn't that right, sweet Moll? And Moll nodded, and the boy clung fast and curled his head into his mother's chest, and still his eyes were closed, and Paddy Gladney felt such a wave of love wash over him that he was nearly knocked to the ground by it, and he put his hand out to steady himself, and he found his wife's hand, and he held it, and she squeezed his hand hard, and he could hear her saying, Thanks be to God, oh, thanks be to God. And Paddy wondered was it the child his wife was thankful for, or the colour of the child, the perfect, unblemished whiteness of this strange flower.

EXODUS

THE HOUSING-ASSOCIATION WOMAN called once or twice a year. She turned sideways at the door to fit herself through it. Mama thought this was funny, as funny as a thing could be. She told Alexander once that the only way she could prevent herself from laughing out loud at the sight of the housing-association woman was to think of her daddy dead in his coffin. Mama was thin back then; Papa was tucked and flat-bellied and handsome. Papa would smile and flash all his teeth at the sight of the housing-association woman and raise his hands flat-palmed, like a preacher lifting his praises to God, pushing his holiness heavenward. Come, come, ma'am, oh, it is good to see you, it is good to see you. Come and see the bureau and the wooden blinds, and the paint on the wall in the young-sters' room. He'd manoeuvre the flushed and massive woman through the kitchen to the back room and he'd turn her and usher her back to the stairwell and he'd point upwards and say, You want to see the upstairs? Oh, my, my, the upstairs has been improved, oh, my, my, the work we been doing, the work.

And the housing-association woman would say, No, it's fine, I'll just make my note in the front room, if you don't mind, and I'll be on my way. And she'd smile and shake her great head in refusal of a drink, a coffee or tea or waiting a while for chicken, rice and peas, because she was always

73

running late and she always had other houses to visit, and Papa would arch himself backwards and frown and shake his head slowly and emphatically from side to side and wring his hands and act as though he could die from this regret, from the shame of having a guest so welcome and of such distinguishment in his house and not being allowed the privilege of serving her something, some small thing, some token of his gratitude and respect and, well, love.

And when she left he'd turn and laugh and say, Woo-hoo, woo-hoo, what a heap of woman, what a huge massive heap, oh, nothing on land or sea that I have ever seen can match the magnificence of that heap of lilywhite woman. And he'd point at Alexander and say, Son, listen well to me now: if ever I'm called to my reward then the charming of that lady-hill is on your shoulders, so mark good the things I do and say when she huff and puff in here to this house. For she is the bridge to the powers that be and our feet must always be firm on her fine planks. And Mama would hit him on his upper arm and chest and tell him to stop his foolish talk, to put away his dirty tongue and thoughts of lady-hills and dying and to give proper example to his daughters and his son.

There was a way of knowing another person's thoughts. It wasn't magic but that's what it would be called by anyone not knowing the working of it. *Magic* was a word bandied about and used as explanation and excuse, promise and threat. People gave signs of what was inside them all the time, without knowing it. Most people were easily read and known. His friend Syd was easy to know. They were as close as brothers. Syd's family lived in the house joined to the left side of Alexander's house, and every word spoken or shouted or screamed in Syd's was heard in Alexander's house, and Alexander's sisters would act out in the evening for Mama and Papa the eavesdropped dramas of the day. Akeelia would be Syd's father and Tasha would be Syd's mother and all of the next-door children together, darting about in front of them, curling herself into a ball when Akeelia whisper-roared in her exaggeration of Syd's father's accent and his booming shout, DIS NOT WHY I LEFT PARADISE BEHIND! I DINT TAKE NO BEATINGS FROM NO POLIS FO DIS! DIS NOT WHY I COME ACROSS THE SEA LIKE A SLAVE! WHY I STOWED AWAY LIKE A RAT! NOT FOR DIS, NOT FOR DIS, DIS, RUBBIIIIIII-ISH! CLEANSE YOUR MOUTHS, CLEANSE YOUR MOUTHS, GET OUT, OUT, OUT OF MY HOUSE! And the Elmwood parents would laugh until their eyes watered, and slap their hands across their hearts and Alexander would laugh along guiltily. Papa would shake his head and say, Oh, Honey Boy Bartlett, what noises you make, what noise, and he'd lean back in his chair and raise his eyes and clasp his hands together in a parody of prayer and declare, A fool gives full vent to his spirit, but a wise man quietly holds it back. Proverbs. Twenty-nine eleven.

Syd would slink across the partition wall in the evenings and wait by the back door of the Elmwood house until he could gain entry. He never knocked, because knocking was asking, and Syd Bartlett didn't ask nothing of nobody. Syd would move about the Elmwood house like a draught, winding silently between the narrow spaces and the people it contained, his love for all of them as clear in his eyes and the inclinations of his head and the movements of his hands as the blueness of the sky between the clouds, and as easily heard in his silence as the hiss and rush of guttered rain. Honey Boy Bartlett had been a bantamweight boxer and his fists flew sometimes of their own accord; his children and his wife knew to duck and weave and retreat when necessary. He'd been beaten with a truncheon outside a nightclub in Hammersmith after his last prize fight. The policeman who'd struck him claimed Honey Boy was involved in an affray; Honey Boy said he'd been trying to break it up. Whatever the truth of it, he went home to his wife and young family untreated, irrevocably altered, no longer fully in charge of his emotions or the volume of his voice.

Alexander's father would watch his wife as she babied their son. You will spoil that boy, Delilah. You will spoil him for the world. How's he ever gonna take a knock? How's he ever gonna pick himself back up off the ground to fight if you keep him baby soft this way? My mama never spoke this way to me, I promise you that. My mama never told me I was the beginning and the end of all that's in Creation, the shiniest star in Heaven. Woo-ee, no. She went at me with a broom handle one time, though. Broke it clean in two offa my back she did. I couldn't stand up straight for a week. I couldn't lie down neither. I was bruised from the cheek of my arse to the back of my head. For my dirtiness, she said it was, though I wasn't doing nothing dirty at the time. I spied you looking at your cousin up and down, she told me. And I spied her shaking herself from her hips at you, God be merciful, God spare her from the devil that be living inside of her, directing her to foulness. That's how soft and praiseful my mama was, Alexander. Everything boiled down to a battle between good and evil, between God and his brother the devil. If you were on the side of good you were left to go about your day unmolested. If you wandered across the invisible line to Satan's side you got a broomstick busted across your spine. Woo, boy, was she tough, my mama, but I loved that woman, save me from harm but I did. And never did I hear such words from her as I hear spoken in this house to my only son, and it's my shame and failing that I let it happen, and my mother is looking down from Heaven where she commands God's kitchen and you can mark it that she's saving up my failings for the day we meet again. And she gonna bust all sorts of heavenly brooms across me.

But Alexander knew his father was full of talk, that he loved to listen to his wife's songs of love, that he loved him just as much as she did, and his sisters too, though he ragged and raged and declared them daily to be Hell-bound. Alexander Elmwood lived his childhood years suffused in love.

Alexander felt a curious desertion of his insight the day he first saw Moll Gladney. She was, in her paleness and smallness and seeming fragility, possessed of a heaviness of spirit, a darkness. She was inscrutable to him, the strange cadence of her speech, the habit she had of looking first above a person's head and then down at the floor before them, and clasping her two hands together as though to steady herself, to tighten her grip on herself, to ward something off. What, he couldn't imagine. Her wide eyes flashed no signs, contained no giveaways; her movements were restrained and careful and economical – she seemed to float around the hotel dining room in the long old-fashioned outfits they made the tea-maids wear, like a ghost. He couldn't speak to her in the small canteen where the workers' staggered breaks were taken, and she hardly looked in his direction once. Until one day she dropped her cup and it smashed across the stained cement floor, and some of the boiling tea it had contained scalded her hand. He stood reflexively and took her by the elbow and led her to the deep sink and ran cold water from the tap over her scarlet skin, and she didn't resist him, and there was a faintly bitter smell from her, masked by some cheap sweetness, and there was something else underlying these scents, something earthy and rich, and he wondered at the sudden lack in himself, of words, of knowledge of what to do or say next. I'm okay, she was saying, I'm okay. You can let go now. And he jumped back as if startled, apologizing, and he looked around and saw that they were alone in the canteen, and he took a brush and dustpan from the corner closet and set to the task of gathering the fragments of teacup from the floor, and he mopped at the spilt tea with a sponge, though most of it had seeped into the cracks and pores of the well-trodden cement, and she sat holding her left hand in her right hand, and she smiled at him when he looked at her and said, You're very good. And he offered to make her a fresh cup of tea and she smiled again and said, That'd be lovely.

He walked her home to her lodgings that day, in a biggish house in Ladbroke Grove, with a high privet hedge in front of it, scaffolded by wrought-iron railings. She walked the half-hour briskly, in almost complete silence, telling him several times that she'd be okay from here, he needn't come the whole way, or have bothered to come any part of the way at all. He told her it was dangerous to walk alone. She seemed surprised at this, and she opened her mouth as if to say something, then seemed to think better of it. She didn't know the danger she was in. Or maybe she knew and didn't care. He started to swap his shifts around so that they mostly matched hers, especially if she was working late, so that he could walk her home. She didn't know that she'd been spotted walking alone in Holland Park and Kensington Gardens, that she'd been seen wandering in Portobello Market. She didn't know that she was stalked sometimes by wolves. That there were marshes on the skirts of the city that had swallowed sins far worse than any she could conceive of committing herself.

She was in some ways a baby in a crib, soft and ripe and incapable of its own protection, ignorant of anything but its own hunger, its own longing. In other ways she seemed ancient, omniscient, burdened by great wisdom. She spoke in short sentences and her words were clipped sometimes and other times drawn out with an upward note at the end, and he'd have to wait until they settled on his ears to know their meaning, and her eyes would meet his and travel up and down him with laughter in them, and he'd feel vulnerable and foolish and as happy as a child. He came, across a plane of months and effort, to know some things about her that in other people he would divine in seconds. That she had run away from something. That she was in love with someone. That she wasn't sure of the truth of herself, or of her own existence, that she thought sometimes this life was all a dream and soon enough she'd wake from it and take up the living of her real life. He came to know for sure one soft and misty day that he loved her, that his love for her was as strong as any love ever was, and as hopeless. He told her that he loved her and she laughed.

Every man is cut a certain way, his father told him. Every change he makes requires a cut that makes him smaller. Ain't no adding things on. That's why you always got to be your own man, son. Be as good a man as ever you can; don't flinch from your goodness. Jesus even said it. And before Him all the prophets. Hear the psalm now, son, the instruction of God: Blessed is the man who walks not in the counsel of the wicked, nor stands in the way of sinners, nor sits in the seat of scoffers; but his delight is in the law of the Lord, and on his law he meditates day and night. He is like a tree planted by streams of water that yields its fruit in its season, and its leaf does not wither. In all that he does, he prospers. Don't be no one else's man but just your own, ever and always.

Alexander cursed his memory, his minute logging of his father's words, his inability to shake the feeling that he was reducing himself by loving this girl who barely looked at him, who gave nearly nothing of herself, who acted sometimes as though she didn't even like him. He felt his temper rising sometimes, when he touched his fingertips to the side of her hand as they walked or pressed his palm lightly against her arm or her side and she flinched or stepped sideways away from him; he felt like shouting at her to fuck off then, to walk on her own, to deal with the grifters and the spivs and the wide-boys herself, and the women who'd slash her face and throat for her red lips, her blue eyes, her neat cut and figure, her whiteness. He felt like shouting at her for being so stupid, for walking like a lamb around these wicked streets with her face made up in powder and rouge, like something from his mother's girlhood, or his grandmother's even, for not noticing the smirks and sniggers of the people around her, for pretending not to wait for him at the staff entrance, searching in her bag for her gloves or her cigarettes or lighter, saying, Oh, hello, Alexander, when she saw him, allowing him barely a smile. The police could stop him on the street, truncheon him in the head, like they did once to Syd's old man, so that he'd lost his grip on himself and spent his time roaring and raving at his sons and daughters in a terraced house in Notting Hill, screaming the brokenness of his heart at them, for some paradise he thought he'd lost. It didn't seem to him as though she'd care terribly were that to happen, and yet he lived each moment of each of his days for her, for the opportunity to talk to her, to be near her, to watch her moving around front of house or sitting primly in the canteen drinking her tea, to hear her soft voice and her strangely lilted syllables, to hear her laugh. He'd cut himself down to a shape smaller than himself; he'd lost himself in love for her.

Her passion shocked him when it came. A spilling, it felt like: no way to recover it, water on cement, splashed once and soaked away, like the tea from Moll's cup that first day. They made love afterwards over the years, and sometimes she even seemed to quite enjoy it, but never with the ferocity and suddenness and intensity of that first time, in her small room in her boarding house, after she'd smuggled him in through the back alleyway and the scullery window. She'd clamped one hand across his mouth and one across her own. She'd sighed afterwards, and he'd thought her sigh was one of contentment, but then she'd turned away from him and cried, and he was suddenly aware of the thinness of the walls of this house, of the length of him in her bed, his feet and ankles poking into air, his trousers on the floor, his shirt still on, two of its buttons gone. He didn't know what to do or say; she gave him no help or guidance or hint. His intuitions all drew a blank. He put his hand on her shoulder and he kissed her right ear and he told her that he loved her. All she said, in the barest of whispers and without turning towards him, was Oh, Alexander. I'm sorry. And he dressed and left without asking her what she was sorry for. He climbed the back wall and slipped down the alleyway and half ran through the echoing streets to the little house in Notting Hill, through a cold misting rain, towards his mother and his father and his sisters and their warm, uncomplicated love.

She told him she was pregnant on a Tuesday. He asked if she was sure and she said she was. She'd been regular to the minute since she was thirteen. She was sick in the early mornings and tired all the time. She told him in a flat voice, while she tied the strings at the front of her uniform, her long fingers working precisely and quickly, without looking at him. They were standing in the archway at the entrance to the restaurant, near the front desk. She didn't seem to care who heard. She asked him what he was going to do. I'll marry you, he said. Fine, she said, and that was that. He was aware that he should move, make some gesture that would lift this exchange from cold transaction but before he could light on an appropriate action she took his right hand in both of hers and raised it to her lips and kissed it, and he thought of Christ, and His anointing in the Jordan by His fiery cousin John, and he saw in her eyes when they met his some new quality of light that he hadn't seen before, and some of the mystery of her was gone, replaced with a sense of some holy purpose that was being ascribed to him, of Fate binding him, holding him fast in place.

He went about the breaking of the news all wrong. As soon as he had said the words, he knew he'd picked the wrong time, the wrong place, the wrong tone. He should have waited until evening time, until they'd eaten, until Akeelia and Tasha were there to absorb some of his parents' shock, so that the wild news would be spread wider, distributed more thinly, dissolved more quickly. He was surprised at himself for failing so completely at this important task. Moll unbalanced all of his equations.

He told his mother in the morning, early, before leaving for the breakfast shift. She was winding her headscarf in front of the mirror in the hallway, preparing to leave for her cleaning job at Hammersmith Hospital. His father was in the bathroom upstairs. His sisters were both in bed, not yet risen for school. Mama, he said to his mother's living back, to her reflected face. Yes, my love? I'm getting married. To a girl from work. She's Irish. She's pregnant. His mother stopped winding; her hands were still, above her head. Pregnant for who? For me. Sweet Jesus Lord, she said, and rolled her eyes so far towards Heaven that only the whites showed. She ceased the winding of her scarf so that it floated to the floor and she covered her mouth with both of her hands then formed them into fists across her chest and dropped to her knees on the threadbare hallway rug. Come on, Mama, stop this, he said. Bar-neeeey, she cried, Bar-neeeey, Bar-NEEEEY. Come, come, hear what this boy has done to us, oh, what a boy we have reared, what a sinful boy, the devil take our boy from us and leave us . . . this.

And his father descended the stairs to the halfway point in his vest and drawers, his face foamed for shaving, his razor in his hand. What is it, woman, what is it? What the boy do? What you do, boy? You kill someone? Police coming? What is it? What? And his mother howled from the floor. He . . . get . . . a girl . . . pregnant . . . a young girl . . . a WHITE girl . . . Oh, my heart, my poor, poor heart. Oh, said Barney, thank the Lord. At least he not kill someone. Akeelia and Tasha were up now, nightdressed and wide-eyed, looking down at him from behind their father. What's going on? GET BACK TO BED, Mama screamed, and they started, implausibly, shockingly, to cry in unison, long keening cries, and Alexander felt angry towards them for the first time in years, since he was a boy and they were usurpers of his princedom, of his parents' unadulterated love.

SHUT UP, he roared. YOU SHUT UP, they roared back, concomitant in rage. Hold on, Barney asked, how young is this girl? She's twenty-one. Oh. She's no girl, then. She's a woman. Still you sinned, though. And you're stuck with that sin now, son. Heed Deuteronomy: should a man meet a virgin and lie with her she shall be his wife and he may not divorce her all his days. And Ephesians: Therefore a man shall leave his father and mother and hold fast to his wife, and the two shall become one flesh. His mother had regained her feet and was standing at the foot of the stairs, one hand on the banister top, and she was shouting, Shut up, husband, shut your stupid, stupid face! What's the good book got to say about bastard children, huh? I'll tell you, you fool: FOR THEIR MOTHER HAS PLAYED THE WHORE SHE WHO CONCEIVED THEM HAS ACTED SHAMEFULLY FOR SHE SAID I WILL GO AFTER MY LOVERS WHO GIVE ME MY BREAD AND MY WATER MY WOOL AND MY FLAX MY OIL AND MY DRINK. Alexander's father looked thoughtfully at his wife and then smiled, and said, You know, Delilah, I think sometimes we know too much of that good book and not enough of the world. Times change and life charges hard. We can't seek to keep up with it no more. We must stand aside and let it pass. Son, bring your girl home and we will welcome her.

They married in a church in Notting Hill. Saint Francis of Assisi, a good saint's name. Barney and Delilah said they didn't mind it being a Roman Catholic church. Why would they? Any place that God was loved and feared was fine by them. The priest was kind and didn't ask the reason for their haste; nor did he ask for letters guaranteeing their freedom to wed. He simply read the marriage rites, blessed their union, and signed the register beneath their signatures, inviting Barney and Delilah forward to witness the transaction, and that was that. An organist played a soft, whirling melody, something that reminded Moll of home, and the priest asked them to sit a while. He pointed at the sacristan, who was carrying the register towards the sacristy door. That man, Jim, is from Mayo. He came here in the twenties as a bare chap of a lad. He's never once been home. All his people now are gone, bar a brother, last he heard. Imagine living that long so far from home, and yet so near to it. It's only a hop, these days. To home, I mean. You can take an aeroplane for a week's wages. The priest looked at Alexander, then at Barney and Delilah, and lastly at Moll, and his eyes fell to her stomach, and she put her hand instinctively across her tiny swelling. Life is life, the priest said. Any sin can be forgiven. The organist just then emerged from a small door to the side of the nave, and they saw that she was walking with a stick, and wearing tinted glasses. Thank you, Martha, the priest said, and the blind woman nodded towards the altar and clacked along the side-aisle towards the door. Martha came as a favour to me. It would have been a colder day without her, don't you think? Whatever about having no guests, you couldn't do without music at so beautiful a moment. This moment you'll only have once. And he looked again from Alexander to Moll and down at Moll's protecting hand, and he followed his lonely Mayo man to the sacristy door.

The baby was born and it was a boy, and everyone was shocked at his whiteness though no one remarked on it at the beginning, and they named him Joshua, and Delilah thought that this was a fine name for a boy, and Barney agreed. It is a name that bears the message that Jehovah saves. He was a good baby, quiet, quick to suckle and to wind and to sleep. He had his father's lips and ears and worried brow; he had his mother's eyes and nose and her pale skin. Oh, the paleness of his skin. So pale that the blueness of his little veins showed starkly through. Syd Bartlett whistled softly through his teeth when he first saw Joshua and he chuckled down at him and said, Little saltfish, who spawn you? And Alexander stood and put his hand on his friend's chest and pushed him towards the doorway, and Syd put out his hands in a gesture of contrition and his eyes flashed with surprise and fear at his friend's sudden anger. Say sorry, Alexander said. To Moll and to Joshua.

And Syd did as he was told, leaning down to where Moll sat before the window of the tiny front room, cradling Joshua, and she could see that he truly was sorry, and that there were tears in his eyes. I'm sorry, Moll. And he touched his palm to the baby's cheek and kissed him gently on the forehead and said, I'm sorry, little man.

They were packed together in the house, with Akeelia and Tasha tucked into the box room that once was Alexander's, and Moll and Alexander and little Joshua billeted in the girls' old room. Akeelia and Tasha seemed besotted with their nephew: they sat with him for hours at a time and were attentive to their new sister. The house was full to bursting and its walls were wet with condensation and it rang with noise, except when Joshua was asleep, when they'd pad shoeless about and speak in the lowest of whispers. Honey Boy blew up one early afternoon, shouting at the rain to go away, cursing God for the wetness of the world he found himself living in: FUCK YOU, RAIN, WEEPING ON MY HEAD, WEEPING, LORD PLEASE SEND ME SUNSHINE TO DRY MY TEARS, OH WHY MUST I DWELL IN THIS VALLEY OF TEARS, OH LORD, WHY HAVE YOU FORSAKEN ME, PLEASE DELIVER ME BACK TO THE LAND OF MY FATHERS, LIFT ME FROM THIS FOUL AND SOAKING PLACE. Delilah Elmwood set a stool against the dividing wall in their backyard and hefted herself onto it and shouted at the top of her strong lungs: HONEY BOY BART-LETT, YOU GONNA BE HAVIN' A COMEBACK FIGHT IN A MINUTE AND YOU GONNA BE KNOCKED OUT COLD I SWEAR. NOW SHUT YOUR FACE YOU CRAZY MAN, YOU KEEPING MY LITTLE GRAND-SON FROM HIS SLEEP. And Honey Boy shouted that he was sorry, and there was silence from next door, and later that evening a bag of coal was lowered from the Bartlett yard into the Elmwood yard.

Alexander watched his new wife closely, to try to gauge what she might be thinking, how she might be feeling. She smiled sometimes but the light in her eyes never changed; her voice was always soft and no intonation or phrase of hers gave him any clue as to what was inside her. She slept well at night between feeds and she thanked him when he changed the baby and took the soiled nappies downstairs and rinsed them in the sink, and she'd be asleep when he got back and he was loath to wake her. He wanted to ask her how this had happened, how he was a married man now and a father, what her part in all this was. How much of this she'd known was going to happen. When he nestled close to her she never moved, but neither did he feel unwelcome, and she smiled sometimes in her sleep, and stirred when the baby stirred, and he'd rest on his elbow and watch them both, and listen to their breath, softly chimed, as though they breathed as one.

He wondered at the universe's precise ordinations, how it seemed necessary for balance always to be achieved. He could read the ebbs and flows and eddies of any water, and this ability allowed him a peaceful life, a steady job; people felt about him a familiar warmth, an eagerness to share their burdens, to help them. He almost always knew what best to say or do in any given situation; he could read any set of circumstances and the aspect and bearing of the actors involved and know where and how to manoeuvre himself, what best to do or not do or say or not say to steer things towards a pacific conclusion. He could read the signs of anyone but those of his own wife. As though the gift he had been given with one hand was removed by the other. He was shocked, though he'd known all along the truth of it, to hear his mother say, That girl is sad. That girl is sad, sad, my son. She got something heavy inside of her, burdening her. Maybe she's missing her mama. Her people. It's not right she hasn't even written them a letter yet. I asked her and she just shook her head. No-oh, she said. And that was it. And another thing, Delilah said. How you gonna raise that boy round here? Syd Bartlett ain't gonna be enough protection, for all the hard men he friends with. That boy too white for being the son of a black man, perfect as he is.

Alexander felt like a child, then, and not a man of twenty-three, a man of six feet two inches, a father. He considered the world beyond the door, teeming with people, the susurrating, unpredictable, dangerous world, the cold concrete scape of the city, the flowerless fields, the deep fast-running river, and he felt the weight of all the dangers posed to his child and his wife collected together, forming themselves into a dark mass drawing in his spirit and light, and he knew he had to retreat before he was consumed by fear.

He felt foolish when Moll left. He should have known it would happen. He came home from work one late afternoon and she was gone. His mother was sitting at the kitchen table with Joshua, feeding him from a teated bottle. At least she'd waited until he'd been weaned. His father sat across the way, his hands beneath his chin, his reading glasses low on his nose. There was a piece of paper in front of him on the table. We thought she going to the shops, son. Or to the hotel maybe to ask about getting her job back. We didn't see her take her suitcase. She gone back to her people, son. Guess she missed them more than she let on. Guess she loved them after all. She left this. And Barney held the crumpled page up before lowering it to the centre of the table. Delilah was shaking her head, smiling down at her grandson, silent save for a low soothing hum, a lilting tune, a shanty. He strained for the memory of it, for the sound of his father singing it in his childhood, for the words of it. How defiant that would be, to ignore the letter and just to break into song, to take his son in his arms and sing to him, a song from the land of his fathers, and send the boy to sleep or, better, to make him smile, to make him lock his eyes on his and light up with recognition and happiness. He felt nothing but rage towards the letter, towards whatever words were on it, towards the hand that had written it.

We're gonna let it lie, son, let it lie awhile. Moll's gone back to that green hill she come from. Be like a holiday for her. Women sometimes lose themselves after babies come. That right, Delilah? And his mother nodded, Mm-mm. Mm-mm. For sure that's right. I'll tell you something now, Alexander, tell you a secret no living person but your papa know. I told it to my mama in a letter before she died, and she wrote straight back to me that it happen to her too. I considered seriously running away from everything after you come to this life. I looked once or twice into the great river in the city and its water was high and deep and I say to myself I could be gone real quick, from everything. All sorts of things happen in a woman's body and a woman's mind when she have a baby. The world seem upside down and not to make sense and sometimes it feel as though she'd be better off separate from her baby and her baby better off separate from her. But always it passes, this madness, it only visits for a brief while. It's not a thing that can last, else no woman ever have a second child and slowly all the world die out. It's like a punishment for some invisible sin, something done long ago. Woman pay a long and heavy price for something done at the dawn of time underneath a tree in Paradise. Woman paying for the sin of Man, all alone she paying. Moll knows this. She gonna come back and if she don't we go to her. That okay, my baby boy? And

Alexander nodded, and was surprised at the taste on his lips of the salt of his own tears.

Alexander woke on his first day in Moll's house with a pain drilling through the centre of his forehead. He had a blurry memory of making it to the town of Nenagh, of checking into a bed-and-breakfast, of making his plan for finding Moll the next morning, of asking some wide-eyed and red-faced people in the café below the bed-and-breakfast if they knew of any Gladneys in the area, of policemen calling to the door of the bed-and-breakfast, of raising his voice to the landlady, who he presumed to have called them, of being told to leave and going to the bar next door, of drinking pint after pint of stout, bought for him by a group of men who stared at him and laughed and clapped his back and asked him all sorts of questions, and there being some sort of misunderstanding and then a set-to, and being rescued by a man who turned out to be Moll's father, and of being driven out of the town and along a narrow road and up a hill to a cottage that looked like something out of a film. Moll had been furious with him when he arrived, but then had taken his hand in hers, and had been tender towards him. He couldn't understand at first what she was saying, or asking, and neither could he form clear answers for her. Why are you here? Where's Joshua? Why are you drunk? And he told her eventually where his parents were, in a hotel back up the road, that they'd bussed it over, all four of them, and that he'd come ahead to find her, and that Joshua was waiting with his parents in the hotel. She darkened with rage, her eyes flashed and burnt; she bared her teeth like an animal. Why can't you just leave me alone? Leave me fucking be, Alex. What do you want from me? And she started to cry then, huge con-vulsing sobs, and he sat on the edge of the bed watching her cry, and he took her in his arms, and she let him, and she said in a whisper, Oh, Alex, what am I going to do? What am I going to do?

He hated himself in that moment for loving her so much. He told himself it was because of their son, that his love for Moll was just the reflection of this holy, consuming thing he felt for the boy, that it was Nature's trick to make a man feel this way about the mother of his children, so that he protects her from harm, so that she'll survive to bear more children, so that the species propagates through the ages. But he knew this wasn't true, that he would have loved her anyway, even had she been barren, that he'd have been as big a fool if she had given him nothing at all, that he'd have followed her to this wild green place on his own, a desperate pilgrim, a flagellant, a clown. Akeelia and Tasha had cried as they were leaving, and begged him not to go. The memory of their pleas cut him now. He told them he'd be back, that Moll had needed a rest from things, and to see her family, and that they'd all be back within the week. But he'd known as he'd spoken those words the untruth of them, that he was leaving behind everything he knew, his sisters and his friends and the street where he'd been born, his job and his plans to study engineering at night, Syd and Honey Boy, and Honey Boy's booming, tormented voice. He'd felt an ache in the centre of his chest and up into his throat as he'd left his parents standing close together in their best clothes at the front of that hotel, left them to voyage back to London on their own, back to the small house that would seem big and empty now to them, and he wished he'd never set eyes on this thin white girl whose expression he couldn't read, whose heart he couldn't know.

Moll's parents were shocked at their sudden grandparenthood, and embarrassed by the sudden presence in their house and in their lives of a tall black stranger. He could feel their discomfort thickening the air of the cottage. He resolved to say as little as possible, to allow them to adjust. He had nothing to say anyway. He'd brought his son so that he'd have a mother, and he was here to have a wife, to live with her as God intended. He wondered if his invocation of God's will would impress them and judged quickly that it wouldn't. He guessed that their faith was as fervent as his parents' but quieter: he didn't think that they'd shout Bible verses at one another in an argument, or that they'd have many arguments at all. Kit seemed always to be on the point of laughing; Paddy seemed always to be about to say something, and then deciding against it. They didn't seem able to sit in his presence, but moved around behind him arranging things, tidying things away or taking things down from the ancient-looking cupboards along the kitchen's far wall; stoking the huge open fire at the other end; making tea; making sandwiches; asking Moll was the child all right, was he asleep, what time would she have to feed him, would he need to be changed. He could see that Kit was smitten by the child, and that Paddy was no less so, but was less inclined to fuss about him, because fussing, to a man like Paddy, was woman's work.

The greenness of the place. Everywhere greenness, trees heavy with it, hedgerows dappled light and dark and every shade of it, rolling fields of grass and green hills as far as his eye could see, and a lake below them in a silver line and, at the far side of it, below the blue and white and grey horizon, more greenness, more grassy hills and forests. Streams of flowers dazzling through the green along the roadsides and the lanes. Branches drooped with berries reaching out from hedgerows, everything blooming and buzzing and dripping with life. Even the rain had a shimmer of green to it. The dizzying inversion of the ratio of block and concrete to greenness and trees and flowers: it was almost too much. London had its islands of tidy and arranged greenness, compressed on all sides by stone. Here the whole world was a bed of yielding earth and greenness, dotted here and there with grey, laced thinly with winding roads on which cars moved slowly in single file and people walked, and old men in dark suits and white collars and knotted ties and flat caps pedalled creaking bicycles, regarding the world around them imperiously, exchanging in drawling voices the greetings of the day. And then, at night, the heart-lifting brightness of the stars.

Paddy and Kit asked nothing of him but he read Paddy's pause by the door and glance towards him before he left the cottage one morning in that first week as a silent request for him to follow. Good lad, Paddy said, the first time that Alexander rose to accompany him on his morning check of livestock and fences. I have a spare pair of wellingtons for you out in the shed. I have overalls too if you want to put them on but they mightn't fit you great. Arra you'll be grand anyway. If there's dirty work to be done I'll do it. His passing of information was perfunctory, delivered flatly and slowly, as though he were talking to a child. The Jackmans have a Charolais herd. Charolais are a breed of cattle brought here to this country from France.

Dry stock only. For beef. We have no milking to do, thanks be to God. We'd be busy men if they milked! There's sheep too, and it gets busy in lambing season, though the sheep manage away grand themselves for the most part. Still and all, though, we must keep an eye on them. The Jackmans have horses, too, and a track where the horses are run out and trained for racing, away down the far side of this hill and over towards Ballywilliam, but they're nothing at all to do with us. I wouldn't know one end of a horse from another.

From then on he walked the fields with Paddy every morning and evening. It seemed to Alexander as though Paddy felt obliged to bring him on his twice-daily patrols, to teach him the art of stewardship. As though one day he were going to hand over the stewardship of the farm to him, Alexander, as some kind of appropriated birthright. He'd point at things and explain them to Alexander, and instruct him on the performance of tasks in the manner of a man passing down ancient wisdoms, and Alexander supposed that there was no other way for Paddy to frame this strange intercourse in his mind, this relationship he never thought he'd have. He helped him to check fences and gates and to repair them when necessary and count animals. I'll tell you one thing, Paddy said, each time they compared numbers. It's great to have a second pair of eyes, the way I can know for sure my count is true. He helped him to fork hay into round feeders from a trailer pulled behind an ancient tractor. Paddy was a small man and strong, full of talk about the weather and the news and the changing season and the flowers and trees and what was blooming and what was dying, and one cold clear night they helped a ewe to birth a breeched lamb and Paddy instructed Alexander to lean himself across the ewe's neck and shoulder where she lay on a bed of straw so that she wouldn't try to get up. The ewe was shorn pink and she raised her neck and turned her eyes to Alexander, and it looked for a moment as though she was crying and then as though she was smiling, and all he could do was say, Shush now, easy now, and as Paddy pushed his hand into the sheep's body and pulled the lamb pink and white and glistening wet by its hind legs into the world, Alexander felt a clicking into place of things, a feeling that all the strange unexpected things that had happened to him had been moved into alignment by some benevolent all-knowing force, that this small stone building on the land of a rich man in the company of a poor man was exactly where he was meant to be, that his life was unfolding, slowly, strangely, exactly as it should.

He'd had a teacher in school who'd called him and Syd his pair of piccaninnies. Whites and Pakistanis and Nigerians and Jamaicans all had names for each other. He'd been called a coon once by a chef in the hotel. A man he didn't know, who'd just started. Where's that fucking coon gone? he'd heard the man say. He'd missed the service bell and the chef was waiting at the pickup point with a plate in each hand. When they were face to face, the man had said it again. Where were you, you lazy fucking coon? The man's teeth were gritted and his thin lips were drawn back; there was hate in his eyes. Alexander had felt a kind of crawling in his groin, moving up his mid-section, a clamping of his organs and muscles, a tidying away, ready for fight or flight. He recognized his body's reaction, and he let it happen. He put his notebook and his pen in his shirt pocket and he closed his hands to fists and the man began to look uncertain. Alexander felt in his own heart the man's sudden timorousness, the dissolving of his mettle. Put the plates down and come out here and call me a coon to my face, he said. Oh, come on, the man said. It was just a joke. I was just ribbing you, mate. Don't be so sensitive. I talk to everyone that way. I call the Paddies fucking Micks and the Spanish fucking Spicks and . . . Hey, I'm a poet and I didn't know it! The man was blustering now, fake-laughing; he was embarrassed and nervous, his face was reddening and Alexander still hadn't moved and Alexander had three inches on the chef and forty pounds and ten years and he gave serious consideration to teaching the man a lesson but he heard Honey Boy Bartlett screaming through the wall of his memory, poor savaged Honey Boy, truncheoned in the forehead, his brain bruised and ruined.

But here he had no comrade, no family, no Jamaican café, no Sunday school or backroom church, no street of his own people, no Syd swaggering beside him, chest out, head high. His blackness here was as remarkable as his son's whiteness had been in Notting Hill, and all the pain of difference now was his, and this was how it had to be. Everywhere people stared. He pretended to be oblivious but in truth he was always aware of the looking, of the whispered conjecture, of the jokes he knew were being made at his expense, and at the expense of Moll and Paddy and Kit and Joshua, and even of the Jackmans. For the first while he enjoyed his strange celebrity. People talked behind their hands to each other, looked him up and down and then looked away, then looked back again when they thought he couldn't see them looking. Some people were brazen about it, and stared openly, sometimes smiling, as if in expectation that he'd begin some kind of performance any second, some kind of justification for his existence among them; he expected sometimes that people would begin to throw coins at him, as though he were a street performer, or a beggar, some kind of exotic mendicant.

In the shop-cum-pub-cum-post-office in the village once during Lent, a few years after Alexander and Joshua moved over, a man who was drinking at the bar counter lifted a small cardboard coin box with a picture on the front of it of a black child and he shouted, Hey, Kunta Kinte, hey, look at this, we're collecting away here for your lads beyond the way they won't starve! How about that? And Alexander had taken the box from the man's hand and put it back down beside the cash register, and he took a pound note from his pocket and folded it into the slot on its top and he stood in front of the man, looking down at him, breathing through his nose, and he knew that the man couldn't back away or retract the name he'd called him, that he had to save face in front of the other men along the bar and the bird-eyed women in the queue at the shop counter, and the small set-to ended in a stalemate and Alexander walked away with the sliced pan and half-pound of ham that Kit had sent him for squashed in the grip of his right hand.

He'd had only a vague idea of what hurling was. He'd heard men talk about it in the hotel in London. Irish men, of course: no one else would care about a game played only in one country by wild animals. He remembered a porter huddled one September Sunday in the corner of the canteen with a transistor radio pressed to his ear, roaring every now and then, telling the head porter to fuck off every time he beckoned him from the doorway, and finally jumping up and punching the air and howling, with tears on his face. His team had won some big trophy, some final; Alexander didn't know or care but he shook the man's hand all the same and listened as he told him of the victory, at a speed too great for half of his speech to be understood. He remembered the man saying, over and over again, Wa-hoo, boy, wa-hoo, boy, fuck them bastards, wa-hoo, boy.

When a man from the lake road drove up to the halfway stile and parked and walked the grassy lane to the house with a wooden thing like a shortened, blunted hockey stick in his hand Alexander had a sense of what was coming. Here he's on, Paddy said, as though he'd known this would happen, as though this was an arranged assignation, a matched courtship. The man said, God bless the work, and whistled at the waist-high walls of the extension they were building at the back of the cottage, and Alexander and Paddy straightened fully from their labour and the man leant himself against the corner of the old wall and held his weapon before him. Do you know what that is, Alex? Of course he does, Paddy said quickly, as if to save his son-in-law from embarrassment. Why wouldn't he know what a hurley is? Lord save us, isn't he here long enough?

His star rose rapidly then, and blazed through that narrow firmament. The club wasn't senior: they needed to win an intermediate championship to be promoted to the top level. The man from the lake road was called Connie and he drilled him every evening for an hour. Alexander learnt to rise the hard leather ball and swing and hit it, to run with the ball balanced on the end of the hurley, to bounce the ball off the end of the hurley as he ran, to throw it up and hit it on the fly. At training he was shocked at the ferocity with which his

99

teammates tackled him, running into him shoulder down, slamming into his diaphragm so that all of his breath was knocked from him and he lay broken and airless and exhausted on the grass of the pitch. Connie looked down at him and turned to the team and blew his whistle so they'd stop and listen to him. Jesus Christ, lads, will ye hit him fuckin harder in the name of fuck and toughen him up a bit or the Toome boys'll fuckin kill him? And night after night this went on and dozens of people came across the fields and up from the village most evenings to Kilcolman to stand on the side-line and watch Paddy Gladney's black son-in-law be savaged like a Spartan recruit, like a prisoner of war, like a condemned man in an amphitheatre, tormented by lions and wolves. Lord, the spectacle of it. Who'd believe it? It was the kind of thing that would do a heart good.

He was awkward but fast. Connie told him that his first touch was a disgrace. Alexander laughed at this. A disgrace to whom? To what? All the other boys and men on the team had played this game since they could walk, had spent every day of their lives practising, could catch and hit the ball without thinking, pass it without looking, dodge around their opponents by pure instinct. And still some older men on the side-lines and in the small stands, like bike sheds, screamed abuse at them. He'd never heard anything like it. GO ON AWAY TO FUCK OUT OF IT YE CUNTS. GO HOME TO FUCK AND ATE YER DINNER. WHAT ARE YE FUCKIN DOIN? MARK UP TO FUCK! WAKE UP YE BOLLIXES! And women too, screaming, all sorts of advice and abuse. And the players on the other teams acted as though they wanted to kill him, flattening him onto his back every chance they got, swinging their hurleys at his legs and stomach and arms and back so that he finished his first match covered with pain. Paddy said he was lucky he wasn't killed. Give it up to hell, son. It's not worth it. It was only a pipe dream of Connie's. He had it in his head you'd be able to pick it up easily on account of being black. But Alexander played on for that first spring and summer, and the small parks where the games were played heaved with people, crowds that had never before been seen, all turned out to see the hurling black man. He learnt to dodge the so-called hatchet-men, to receive the ball on the wing and to balance it on the end of the stick, and to run full pelt towards the opposition goal, and to change his direction at the last second, just before the mountainous full-backs killed him, and to flick the ball back to his hand and to throw it and swing at it, to visualize the net shaking before it shook at all, to connect clean and swing through without thinking.

He was no hindrance and he was sometimes, even often, a help. His speed was unmatched. He could make his body go anywhere but not the ball. He could thread himself through a packed defence and into a goalmouth, almost carrying the ball over the line. But he couldn't pass accurately and he couldn't score from outfield: the ball would not lift itself for him or travel in the direction of his eye. They won enough games to be promoted and a party was held in the clubhouse bar on the evening of their last match and he drank stout again for the first time since his lonely night in the Swagman's Inn, and a photographer and a man with a tape recorder asked him questions about his background and how he had come to be in this village, to be a centre forward on this hurling team, and he told the man that he loved this place and these people, and that he was married to the most beautiful girl in Ireland, and his picture was taken with his teammates around him at the front of the clubhouse and the following Sunday he saw himself looking back at himself from the pages of a national newspaper, and Moll was shaking her head and her eyes were closed and she was saying, Oh, Jesus Christ, Alexander, what the fuck did you say that for? The most beautiful girl in Ireland? That is mortifying! And Kit shushed her and told her to mind her language in front of the lad and Paddy rounded a little bit, though he was not as a rule given to anger, and he snapped that she could be called worse things in a newspaper, worse things by far, and she didn't know she was born if she felt hard done by having a husband like Alexander, who'd leave his country and his people behind and take up a life so strange to him, and try his damnedest to fit in and to be someone and to be good, and Lord Jaysus you should be pure solid ashamed of yourself, Moll Gladney.

Connie got him a job in the aluminium factory in Nenagh. The men there were mostly townies: their voices drawled more than those of the villagers; they shouted jokes and insults up and down the lines. He worked a machine with grinding teeth that pressed together on flat panels and distorted them according to the arrangement of the teeth, and the arrangements were copied from plans that were delivered to him daily by a small blonde woman who'd smile at him and stand watching as he set to the task of arranging and setting his machine for the day's work. She's mad for a look at your cock, one of the other men said, and the whole line laughed. She's heard rumours. BIG rumours. And he smiled at the joke and he felt himself burn with shame and he couldn't say exactly why he felt shame, but he tried to narrow himself behind his machine, standing sideways to the line, stooping a little to take an inch or two off his height. He cycled into town and back, unless it was raining hard, and when it was, Paddy would drive him in his old Austin and he'd talk non-stop about nothing much for the full five miles and Alexander wouldn't follow all of it; he loved to let the old man's words float around him, filling the empty space around him, and he loved when Paddy said good-bye at the factory gate, saying, I'll see you later, love. Always love.

Paddy stirred in him a fascination with trees. He'd stop sometimes and put his hand against a trunk and say, Come here, Alexander, feel that. And Alexander would rub the trunk and Paddy would say, Do you feel the knottiness of the bark of that tree? And do you see how wide and round are the leaves? And look the way the trunk is split off into several separate trunks from the wideness at the bottom. That's all a measure of the toughness of this tree, and its usefulness. This is a tree designed by Nature to give quarter to small creatures, to give shelter and succour to things that otherwise would die in the elements. A black alder, it's called. In the old days it was con-sidered a mortal offence to chop down one of these. Oh, God, yes. You'd have been for the chop yourself if you'd done that! There's a cure in the alder, they say, though I wouldn't know now how to go about drawing the cure from the tree. That kind of knowledge is gone with the years. Or he might stop somewhere along the line of oaks near the brow of the hill they lived on and say, You know, Alexander, the thing about an oak tree, the remarkable thing, is this: it can live a thousand years. Every tree along here was here before the Normans came to this country. The only living things in this country that were ever truly free are our ancient oaks! They draw water like demons, they do. They're thirsty out. Signs on they always thrived in this wet country. A birch will weather any kind of drought, it'll live on the dewfall if needs be, but a hundred gallons a day an oak will take up from the earth. And for every million acorns produced by oak trees, do you know how many go on to be oak trees of their own? One. Can you imagine that?

The novelty of Alexander wore off. A black doctor came to work in the hospital, and a brown doctor soon after him, and they had a black wife and a brown wife, and black and brown children, and Alexander Elmwood, Moll Gladney's black husband, was no big deal any more. There was a choice of foreigners to be looked at and wondered about all of a sudden. He was moved from the line to the factory office and there was a bit of trouble from the union but it soon died down. Some of the men called him turncoat in the canteen and someone asked him was he going to be a boy for the Fitzwilliam family, and he found himself eating his lunch alone for a while, but they soon realized that he was in charge of wages, and that he never made a mistake with his calculation of overtime the way his predecessor often had, and that there was never an argument about clocking cards being short minutes and there was never a delay with holiday pay or bonuses or double-time for bank holidays, and with the settling of time came happiness that their mate Black Alex was in the office, looking out for them.

Lucas Jackman asked him to landscape his front lawn. Alexander was surprised at this. Lucas Jackman had always treated him with aloofness, with something approximating contempt. He knew that Lucas Jackman was the kind of man who valued only other wealthy men. But he was straightforward in his request, and plain about his reason: he wanted the garden to look well; he had regular guests with whom he did business and an attractive, well-kept garden generated the right sort of image, put people in a certain frame of mind. He knew that Alexander had done some landscaping work with Paddy and he saw how well he kept the garden at the cottage, and the hedgerow along the boreen. Alexander planned the garden out with Paddy's advice and he showed his rough sketch and notes to Ellen Jackman before he started and he applied for a week of leave from the factory. He ringed the garden with a well-spaced boundary of poplars, with lilac and wild crab-apple starring inwards towards the centre. He created an inner circle of carmines, delphiniums and lupins, around a shallow, heart-shaped rockery in the very middle, with cyclamen and poinsettia and jasmine, so that the garden would have colour in winter. Paddy helped him to make a love seat from the trunk of a wind-felled tree and he set it against the garden's end wall, and along the wall he trellised roses. He sat with Moll one late spring evening on the love seat as his work on the garden was finishing and she told him that the garden was beautiful, that he was after making something really, really beautiful. Not for the first time, she said, and smiled at him, a rare smile. I love you, Moll, he said. I love you too, she whispered, without looking at him, and in that moment he believed her.

His mother wrote to him to say that his father was dying and he flew home with a day to spare, and his father squeezed his hand hard and said he was proud, as proud of his son as a man could be. And a few years later Akeelia rang the post office and left him a message to say that Mama was on her way to the Promised Land to be with Papa and he didn't make it home in time to say goodbye. Moll came with him on that trip and she was good to him and she was good to Akeelia and Tasha and their husbands and children, and she arranged the distribution of Mama and Papa's furniture and the division of their poor estate and the handover of their home to the housing association, and Alexander was surprised to see the same massive lady in the job, not quite as big now, even slower on her feet, just as rosy-cheeked and anxious to be through the house and out again. As she left she turned to Alexander and said, Your parents were fine people. And she took his hand in hers and held it for a while and he could see a tear at the corner of her eye.

The factory closed and he went into business on his own. Lucas Jackman pressed his friends to consider him when they needed landscaping done. He found himself in demand. Lucas Jackman insisted on paying for equipment for him, a good geared mower and a solid trailer and a new chainsaw and industrial strimmer, and Alexander was embarrassed at this largesse, but Lucas said he was to consider it a business loan, at a low rate and over a long term. But whenever Alexander went to pay him back any part of the money, Lucas Jackman would refuse it. Paddy and Kit advised him to put it aside, the way he'd have it to give, for fear Lucas's weather would suddenly change. Paddy helped him when he had a heavy job, and advised him on the kinds of plants that complemented one another and the kinds that set themselves in competition against each other. He learnt to draft properly and he set up a drawing table in the shed beside the cottage. He gained a reputation for reliability and innovation and value, and after a season or two, it seemed that every posh house in five parishes had an Elmwood garden.

Every clement Friday they picnicked at the cottage. Moll would lay a spread along a blanket in the soft grass by the side of the orchard entrance, in a sunny spot cooled by the dappling shade of the branches of the biggest of the trees, and he'd walk up the laneway to the sound of their laughter, to the sound of Joshua shouting, Daddy! Daddy! I see Daddy! And the boy would run to meet him by the garden gate and he'd bend to kiss him and they'd sit on the ground in the orchard, Moll, Joshua and him, and sometimes Paddy and Kit and sometimes Ellen Jackman, and they'd drink tea and eat triangled sandwiches and apple tart and currant buns, and Joshua would tell them the stories of his day, of the poem that he'd heard in school about the lonely giant, of the ladybird he'd made friends with on the laneway, of the girl who'd borrowed his colouring pencil and broken it but he didn't mind because he was going to marry her, about the fifty pence that Lucas Jackman had given him when he'd called earlier. And the years glided along like this and Joshua became less inclined to tell stories and more inclined to write them down and hide them in his bedroom, and they had to draw him out and eventually he'd let them in on some of his secrets: how he wanted to be a writer, how he'd held hands with a girl but he hadn't kissed her, how okay he'd kissed her but not on the lips, okay on the lips but with their mouths closed and only for a few seconds, and they'd listen and laugh and feel the sun on their faces and the sweet-scented breeze, and Moll would shine with happiness, and Alexander Elmwood's heart would be at peace, and the world would spin true on its axis.

SONG OF SONGS

JOSH FEELS A kind of warm peace and a lightness in his being as he walks the cobbled concourse to the edge of the river. It's in flood, high and savage, brown with churned mud. He's going in, boots and all, he's going in. He feels dizzy with relief, with expectation; his fear is momentary, a tiny fibrillation through his ecstasy, easily ignored. The drop from the wall is short, he'll fall forward, break the water head first, in and under, one airless inhale and he'll be gone, gone, and carried with the current to the sea. He raises himself onto the low wall, steadying himself between two fake battlements, and the rush and wash of the river and of his own speeding blood fills his ears. As he closes his eyes and slowly exhales and leans himself outwards he hears a noise behind him, hurried footsteps, a shout. Hey. Hey, what are you doing?

He looks behind him and sees a girl, hands on hips, leaning slightly forward as though breathless, and recognizes her. She'd stood and started towards him just as the audience had begun to heckle him, to hiss and click their tongues and laugh, and he'd seen her face and eyes, and her eyes had been wide and brown and her hair had been pulled back and braided tightly, dark perfect furrows along her head, extending to narrow tails as far as her shoulders. She'd been opening her mouth to speak as he'd started away from the mic, scrunching his poem as he did so, and dropping it. It was in her hand now, he could see. Christ. His fucking stupid poem was in her hand and there was a fair chance she'd have read it while he'd been looking at the water, too chickenshit as always to make his move, to just do it, to jump, to rid the world of himself.

She's smiling now and he's stepped back onto the cobbles and he's standing facing her and he's very aware of his hands hanging at his sides. She's wearing a white T-shirt that billows a little from her body in the breeze, tucked loosely into the waistband of her jeans with a print of Che Guevara on it, and it occurs to him, ludicrously, to tell her that an Irishman made that picture of the hero of the Cuban revolution, a fella from Galway, and he hears himself speaking, but all he's saying is, I was just, just having a look, at the river, like, and she's saying back, It's okay, you don't have to explain, I just wanted to give you back your poem – you dropped it when you were walking off-stage. Jesus Christ, he says, and looks down at her feet, and sees that her blue Converse and the flared hems of her jeans are soaking and mud-flecked to the knees, like she was running through puddles, and he apologizes reflexively for swearing, something is in his head, some dim echo, about some kind of prim religiosity in parts of London, lots of them being born-again Christians or Jehovah's Witnesses or something like that, and when he looks back up her smile has faded and there's a kind of searching, concerned expression on her face, and she's proffering his crumpled poem and saying, It's beautiful. I had a quick read while I was waiting for you. I thought you were in the toilet. Then I saw you in the alleyway and went after you. I love the bit where he shouts at the swans and

112

they ignore him. You should have read it. They would have loved it.

I got nervous, Josh says. He reaches towards her to take the paper from her and sees that his hand is shaking. His hand, he sees, is in her hand. Pleased to meet you, she says. I'm Honey. I've been looking for you.

JOSH IS EMBARRASSED now. Honey is smiling at him from across the table and her hands are lying flat and he can't stop looking at them. The straight narrow lines of her bones extend back from her fingers, converging towards her wrist, an arcing, perfect delta, her long nails painted white, the pucker of skin at her knuckles, the soft mounds around the bases of her thumbs. Her hands are almost too beautiful. Is it possible that something could be too beautiful? Like a mistake was made somewhere, an over-applying of loveliness in one place, a cosmic spillage. Her hands feel dangerous, somehow, like he could be foolish over them, or violent: if someone walked over right now and grabbed one of them roughly he might attack that person; he might get himself killed over these hands.

He's afraid to look up at her face: her face will be too much for sure. Her chin and lips and nose and eyes and forehead and her braided hair he knows are all perfect, but in this moment it would be too much for him to see them, to see her smile; he'd cry like a child or stammer if he tried to speak, or blurt out that he loves her, that he wants to marry her, that he'd die for her. He considers taking one of her hands in one of his. No. Impossible. She's given no signal that he'd be welcome to do so. But they are both lying palms down flat, available, only an inch or so from his own hands. Why can't he be brave?

It's a week since first they met, since she saved his life, he supposes, though that's a thing that lies unvoiced between them, only alluded to in her assurances to him, as she leaves for home every night, that she'll be back the next day, her checking and rechecking that he's all right, that he's feeling okay, the look of relief he'd seen on her face the first day she returned.

The café is closing: the lights are, one by one, going out. The sun is low and autumn-weak and lights the girl's face softly. The owner's voice is booming loud: he's singing as he swings stools onto tables, a song that Josh knows well. *Chi-Chi-bud-oh, Chi-Chi-bud-oh, some a dem a holla some a bawl.* He can't quite believe he's hearing that song, here, so far from home, but after a moment it makes perfect sense. Honey is saying, Come on, we'll walk down by the river, there's another open-mic night on the Embankment, in a different place to last time, maybe you'll read one of your poems tonight? But he shakes his head. He can't imagine trying to read in front of an audience now or ever again. He wants to read only for her; he wants the world to be composed of him and her. He wants to read his story to her, the one about the blind man from the Bible, his alternative gospel; he can't quite believe how desperately he wants to read to her. He wants her to know that he's going to be a famous writer, that she's going to be a famous writer's wife, that they're going to have famous writer's children together, three at least, maybe four or five, the more children the better, so that she'll have to stay indoors and mind them and wait for him to come home from being a famous writer and no one will be able to grab her roughly, to put their hands on her hands or on any other part of her, to snatch her away from him.

You can stay ten more minutes if you want, the owner says

to them. I have to cash up. You relax, eh? Finish your coffee, take your time. And he smiles at them and winks at Josh, and Josh tries to wink back but he does so with both his eyes so that he looks like there's something wrong with him and the man seems puzzled and turns back to his till and his song about birds. Honey knows the café owner well: she's a regular here, her college nearby. There's a silence and an expression on Honey's face of expectation, as though she's waiting for him to say something, or ask something, or reveal something more about himself, some secret thing.

Without knowing he was going to do it he starts to tell Honey about the picnics he used to have with his mother and his grandmother on summer afternoons, how they seemed to last all day, and the school desk he used to sit at, the one his grandfather had salvaged from the old schoolhouse in the village when they built the new school down the road from it. How sometimes their neighbour Ellen Jackman would walk across the meadow from the big house and she and his mother would sit together on a rug spread out on the stretch of grass between the side of the cottage and the entrance to the orchard, where they'd have a clear view down the lane, and his grandmother would carry trays of plates from the kitchen of the cottage with slices of apple tart and cream and buns and tiny round cakes with chocolate icing.

Honey is resting her face on her hands now and her fingers are extended along her cheeks and she's smiling with her eyes as he speaks. She laughs softly here and there and repeats some words in a whisper, words that are unfamiliar to her; he keeps forgetting his voice and his syntax must sound strange to her. I was a fat kid, Josh says, and Honey laughs, and her eyes change now, there's a new light in them, and she says that she can imagine him, that he must have been beautiful. Kids should be fat, she says. Filled with sugar and kindness and love. If I have kids they're going to be enormous. I'll stuff them full of everything they want. And Josh laughs now too and he goes on.

Mam and Ellen Jackman were always laughing at something, jokes they always had between them, and it used to drive Granny mad. Ellen Jackman owned the house we lived in and all the land around it. Or her husband did. So my grandmother always acted a bit nervous around her, and when she left she'd always give out to my mother, saying, Will you conduct yourself properly any more when that one is around? You're a show, so you are. Skitting and giggling like a stupid little schoolgirl. And she's no better. But she has something beneath her and behind her, and you haven't, don't forget. Conduct yourself now, Moll. But Mam would only ever laugh.

We'd wait for my granddad and my dad to come home. Granddad would always arrive first: we'd hear the creaky pedal of his bike long before we'd see him. He was a postman. We'd hear him singing coming up the lane. I'd run down along to meet him and there'd be this fresh, airy smell off him, like he'd been washed by wind. The top of his head was always brown and freckled in summer because his comb-over wouldn't hold on the bicycle. It'd unravel on sunny days because he wouldn't be wearing his cap and it'd fly out behind him. He'd put me on the crossbar of his bike and push me up the hill to home. Then he'd squeeze into my old school desk and Granny or Mam would bring him a cup of tea and he'd take out a hanky and wipe his face and head with it and he'd smile up at the sky and say, Ah, now. Isn't this the life? And he'd tell us all for the thousandth time how that exact desk was the one he'd sat at himself all through primary school and how British soldiers came bursting in one day with guns and made them all stand against the top wall in front of the blackboard and they'd pointed a gun at the master and taken him away because he was after being involved the night before in the shooting-up of the barracks inside in Nenagh and the murder of three police-men, and Granny would cut across him and say, Will you stop telling lies? You weren't even born that time!

And Granddad would clear his throat and declare: I was born in the year nineteen and ten. And with these eyes I have seen some things. Then he'd open his eyes really wide and look down into my face. And with these ears I have heard some things. And he'd pull out the two lobes of his ears and wiggle them about. And with these hands I have done some things. And he'd hold out his two hands and he'd make them into claws and then he'd turn all of a sudden and grab me around the throat and pretend like he was going to choke me and I'd roar with laughter. And I always remember Granny, reacting the same way every single time: Shut up, you eejit. You're blind and deaf and you always were, and you haven't hands to wipe your arse. But she'd be laughing behind it.

Then my dad would arrive, walking up the boreen from the road. And Honey interrupts him. What on earth is a bo-reen? And Josh laughs at the sound of the word from her mouth: it sounds so strange spoken in her London accent, so funny, so sexy. He feels happy in this moment, actual happiness, that the moment he's existing in has the best possible aspect of any moment he could exist in: the best smell and taste and texture and colour and shape; no human could be more beautiful than the human before him; no story could be more enjoyable in the telling than the one he's telling that beautiful human about the picnics of his childhood summers in the orchard; no sound could be more exotic or delicious or fascinating than the sound of her saying *boreen*. What on earth is a bo-reen?

So he tells her it just means *small road*, and he tells her how his father was the first black man most of his neighbours ever saw in the flesh. And Josh stops here because he needs to be careful of his voice. He knows now he won't cry but he hates it when his voice cracks and his sorrow makes his breath catch and his words stop; people look at him with embarrassed sympathy and sometimes put out a hand to rub some part of him, his upper arm usually, and they say things like, Ah, now, now, nonsensical syllables with no anchor and no weight, no power, tiny birds tossed in a hurricane. He starts to tell Honey about his childhood, how it looked and felt, and he sees his father clearly as he talks, his happy face and broad smile, his huge hands, lifting bunches of sapling trees into the flat bed of his granddad's trailer, saying, Come on with me, son, we'll plant these trees and we'll get an ice cream, and he feels the wind on his face in the car because his dad always drove with the window wound fully down, and he can hear him singing the song the café owner, unbelievably, magically it seemed, was just singing, *Chi-Chi-bud-oh*, the call and response song about birds that can be changed every time it's sung.

He hears his father's strong sweet voice, drawing out the last syllable of the refrain, CHI-CHI-BUD-OOOOOOH, and he can hear himself answer, SOME A DEM A HOLLA, SOME A BAWL, and he tells Honey how his father would sing a line, and he sings it for her so she'll know how it went, SOME ARE

BLACK BUD, DEY ALWAYS SINGIN, and he sings the answer he'd have given to his father, SOME A DEM A HOLLA, SOME A BAWL, and his father would sing, SOME ARE SWALLOW, DEY CHASIN FLIES NOW, and Josh would answer again, raising his voice against the rushing wind, up towards the sky and the clouds and sun, and his father would sing, SOME ARE BIGSHOTS, THEY HAVE DE MONEY, and Josh would answer again, and his father would make up new lines, SOME ARE GRANNIES, DEY MAKIN FRUIT-CAKE, SOME ARE JACKMANS, DEY RIDIN HORSES, SOME ARE GRANDDADS, DEY ARE DE POSTMAN, SOME ARE JOSHUAS, DEY LOVE DEY DADDY, and the song would go on and on, all the way in to Nenagh or to Borrisokane or Thurles or even to Limerick city, wherever the garden was that they were working on, and he can see his dad standing in the centre of the site and turning slowly to survey it, measuring his borders and his lines of trees with his eyes first, and then with careful paces, and looking at his sketches and his notes, and arguing with himself, What the blazes, Alexander, what did you mean by that? Oo-ee you are a foolish man! while Josh waits, laughing, saying, Come on, Dad, I want my ice cream, and his dad snapping his heels together and saluting and shouting, SIR, yes, SIR, tally-ho, tally-hoo, the captain wants his ice cream, forward march, left turn, fall in in threes, break out in branches, high-stepping in a circle around Josh, his long legs and arms scissoring and pistoning up and down, in and out, while Josh laughs until he can hardly breathe.

He tells Honey about his earliest memory, of standing in a field of knee-high grass. His mother and his father standing uphill from him, facing him, their hands out to him. The sun behind them and the blue sky. The sound of them laughing, calling to him, Come on, slowcoach, come on. The slope and the heavy grass slowing him as he tries to move towards them, starting to cry, saying, Come back and get me, carry me, I'm tired. As he describes the scene to her he can almost feel his father's hands on him, lifting him, like he was made of paper, onto his broad shoulders. He feels himself unshackled from gravity, he feels the folds of skin on his father's brow beneath his fingers and palms, he feels his father's big hands on his knees, holding him steady as they crest the hill and start down the far side towards the stream, where they'll sit on the ground beneath the alder tree and watch for jumping fish. He sees his mother from this strange angle, the top of her head, the side of her nose and mouth as she walks, the curve of her cheek. He reaches down and touches his hand to her hair and she turns her head and looks up at him, laughing, and says, Hey, you, little fairy man! He hears his father's gentle, rumbling laugh. He feels the pureness of his love for them and of their love for him, the strength of it, as huge and solid as the earth itself.

He tells Honey about his father playing hurling, reluctantly, as a favour to his friend Connie, just for a couple of games, to see the season out. Hurling? He describes to her the game, like hockey, but with a leather ball and you can pick it up, the oldest field sport in the world, and fastest, the sport of ancient kings, and she shakes her head as though he's making this part up. He describes his father, holding his hurley with his right hand low on the grip, an unorthodox style, awkward-looking, faster than anyone on the field but too gentle for the game, too disinclined to swing for fear he'd hurt someone. Surging through from centre-field, throwing the sliotar up and batting it back down, into the back of the net through the legs of the opposition goalie, who runs out to meet him and smashes his elbow into his father's face so that his head snaps back and his legs buckle and he falls to his knees and then forward onto the ground. The goalie shouting as he leans over his father, Fuck you, you black bastard, and the subs and the trainers and some of the spectators breaching the side-line, and the heaviness of dread in his legs as he runs forward towards where his father is lying, and one of his father's teammates wrestling on the ground with the goalie and all the players milling around fighting and there are elbows and fists and knees and legs everywhere, and curses and shouts and words being flung around that Josh doesn't know the meaning of, and everyone, it seems, is hitting someone and he sees his father getting up from the ground and smiling and walking away from the riot, towards the side-line, towards him, and holding out his hand to him and saying, Come on, son. Let's go home. This game is gonna be the death of me. An angry voice from behind him saying, Hey, Elmwood! You can't just walk away! Why didn't you fuckin hit him back? His father holding his hurley out to the man, saying, Why don't you do it for me? And his father laughing, saying, Come on, Little Bud-Oh, let's go and get an ice cream.

The café owner is standing by their table now, taking his apron off, laughing a deep bass laugh, saying, You sing it well. That damn song! It sticks itself in my head some days and I can't shake it off! And Josh feels his embarrassment rushing back, washing in a torrent over him, and he feels his cheeks burn, and he can't believe himself. Talking, talking like this, spilling out his sorrows to this girl in this strange place, this girl he knows so little about: she must think he's a selfish prick,

122

a stupid, self-involved cry-baby, a boy, a lost little boy, pathetic, laughable. She's giving him her time out of some sense of obligation, some duty that has been imposed on her by the shared part of their histories. She's putting her coat on and she's thanking the café owner and he can feel the folded pages of his story in the inside pocket of his own jacket and he thinks he'll burn them when he gets back to the flat, into the sink so that he can easily wash away the evidence, and he can think about starting again, or giving up, giving up, giving up.

JOSH IS LYING on his back on his narrow mattress in his stale flat. The Roscommon lad he'd been sharing with since the start of summer is gone, back to Ireland to work in his father's grocery shop. He misses him. Even though he was a useless fucker, always a few pounds short with his half of the rent, always on the take. Everything suffixed with *een* when it was going in his direction, to diminish his scrounginess, trying to make things seem small, insignificant, easily reciprocated. Gimme a drag*een* of your smoke there, youssir, hye. You couldn't gimme a loan*een* there till I get paid, hye. Hye, boss, can I have a taysht*een* of your pizza, hye. Anyway, he's gone, flitted, and a month's rent owed. Fuck him and his fucking *een*s. Josh has a few weeks more of work in the potwash in The Waverley and he'll flit himself when the work runs out, and the weird bent-backed landlord can take the unpaid rent out of his deposit and fucking sing for the rest. He's alive. He's still alive, after all. He is, unexpectedly, alive and in love. He'll have to see that small thing out, the small, dense, massive thing that has him helpless, desperate, locked in a dizzy orbit of desire.

Josh is happy in the quiet early morning, or peaceful at least, listening to the distant calls of birds above the mumble of traffic, smoking a weak joint, just for the sweet mint taste of hash, and he's half dreaming of a rainy day in early summer, four years ago, or maybe five, just at the start of the holidays, when he'd walked the Shannon callows with a girl, and they'd sat side by side on a spit of sand and reeds by the lake's edge, and they'd taken off their tops, and she'd kissed him on the side of his face, and down along his chest, and she'd stayed going, and he'd looked at the blue sky and the massing clouds and it seemed in that moment that he was being smiled upon by God, applauded by the heavens, and they'd lain afterwards by the whispering lake, looking upwards at the swallows and the gulls, and she'd whispered that she loved him, that he was her man, and his heart had swelled and they'd walked hand-in-hand back to the main road and down along it to her house, and her mother had been there, and the girl had stood holding his hand in their shining kitchen, presenting him, and her mother's eyes had run up and down him, and her lips had pursed and her eyes had creased, and he'd known what she was thinking, could see the images that were flashing in her mind of their tiny cottage on the hillside, and the extension that his father and his grandfather had built behind it, and his thread-bare mother, and his father and his dark brown skin and his ancient suit, the paisley dicky-bow he wore to Mass, his granny and his granddad and their rust-eaten car, their stations and devotions, their poor beliefs. And he knew that she could hear the echoes of gossip and mocking laughter. And he knew he wasn't good enough.

He puts out his right hand to touch the pile of handwritten pages on the floor beside his bed, stapled together, frayed at the edges, stained and blotted here and there with corrections and crossed-out lines. He didn't burn them in the end and now he's glad. He has no copy. He thinks of the story as his father's

125

story; his father gave him the idea for it, and he imagines all the time how his father would have reacted if he'd ever read it. He'd have shaken his head slowly as he read the last line, and looked up to where Josh was sitting watching him read at the far side of the kitchen table, and said something like That's it, son. That's it. That's what I meant when I said there was more to the blind man's story. More than we're told in the Gospel of John. You did it better than the Bible, son. And he'd have laughed, the laugh that started somewhere down deep inside him and broke upwards, and filled a room with sound and light. Josh thinks today he'll read it to Honey. Some of it, anyway.

He doesn't know where this impulse comes from, this strange desire, to read to her words he wrote himself, words he's not sure about, to look up at her face as she listens, maybe with her eyes closed. Maybe he'll embarrass her, put her in an awkward position. What if she thinks it's shit? He's already spilt his guts to her about his childhood, telling her about those stupid Friday picnics, and he feels his happiness retreat as his temper rises again, rises and widens and fills him, and his mother's face is clear now in the smoky haze above him, her blue eyes filled with tears as he screamed at her, screamed, that she was a bitch, that she never loved Daddy, that she never gave a fuck about him, that she was a bitch, a bitch, a bitch.

Honey waits, watching Josh's face. It's been only a week and a day but she knows enough about this boy to know that the best thing she can say when his head is bowed and his pages are in his hand and his eyes are closed is nothing at all. He'll eventually start reading again. And she'll have to breathe in and hold her breath for five or six or seven beats of her heart before exhaling slowly to keep herself from laughing. She'll have to almost suffocate herself in order not to laugh. There's just something about his face, his eyes, the way his lips move when he forms his words, the boyish seriousness of him, the way he tries his best to read slowly, his accent, nothing like she's ever heard before, that makes her want badly to laugh, and she's not sure exactly why, and she knows she can't. She knows he wasn't really looking at the river that day on the Embankment. She knows the danger he was in.

She spent the summer searching for him. Well, watching out for him at least. Ringing friends and describing him, calling at places she was told he might go. When her friend Raymond left a message at the college reception desk saying a Joshua Elmwood with an Irish accent and black hair, just shy of six feet in his Docs, had booked a spot on his poetry open mic she'd felt triumphant. She'd found him. So why shouldn't she keep him for herself for a while? She's never been selfish before in her nineteen years. Not that she can remember, anyway. She didn't even make a fuss when her mother left, just nodded at her promises to see her every week, said, Goodbye, Mum, and that was that.

She senses that he's happy now, or something approaching it. She read the letters from Akeelia in New York and Tasha in Australia and there was no sense of mortal urgency about them. Keep an eye out for Alex's boy. They think he's in London somewhere. He's quarrelled with his mum. Then small-talk for a page or so, and the same photo enclosed with each letter, of Josh's face, a few years ago, at eighteen or nineteen maybe, a passport photo it looks like, pale and unsmiling, squinting slightly so that you can't see how beautiful his eyes are, chin defiantly up. He's not a missing person, more a person missed. Anyway, he's hers for now, her secret thing, her warm comfort, her project. She'll tell her dad she's found him soon enough. She's never seen a boy like this, so soft and earnest, so devoid of awareness of himself, so ignorant of his own selfishness. She wants to shout at him, Wake up, wake up, the world is hard and it rushes on regardless of your heart, and people never take the shape you want them to, people are stubborn about that, about being themselves, even when they're trying to be someone else. No one can hide for ever.

Looking for Joshua Elmwood. She's been composing a screenplay in her head. She has it constructed now scene for scene. She can see it printed, prefaced, bound, submitted as her final project in her film studies course. She can see her tutor's face, hear his words of astonishment and praise. She's going to get an A, a first, maybe a medal. She has it filmed, edited, sold for worldwide distribution; she has the VHS cover designed.

A boy with black curly hair, overlong, partially obscuring his face, brown eyes deep and sad, half turned towards a girl, their hands extended towards each other, fingertips almost touching but not quite, each figure backgrounded differently to show that they're separated by space or time or both. Or maybe it would only go to arty festivals, Cannes, Sundance; maybe it would win obscure but coveted awards. Whichever, she's found him now, by some sweet swerve of Fate, and she still can't quite believe he's real.

She smiles across at him. The pages of the story are on his lap. He read the first few lines to her and she whispered, Oh, God. That's so sad. And he'd had to stop, because her saying that made him feel foolish, as though he'd tried too hard with the first lines, tried to say and do too much, and he wonders again why it's become something close to a matter of life and death for him, the reading of the story aloud to this girl he barely knows, who happened upon him one smoky evening as he stood making a silent wet-eyed fool of himself on a beer-crate stage in front of a crackling microphone in a pub near the Embankment. What had driven him to that place, to that quivering moment? His last stand, it had felt like, something minutely noble as his closing act, some tiny living-out of his fantasy. To be a writer. To declare himself in public to be a writer. And even then embarrassment had stymied him, lack of conviction, worry about the world's opinion of him, the world, compressed into a half-billionth part of itself, ranged dis-interestedly across a few rows of barstools and barrel-tables in a backstreet London pub, river-rats sniffing at its damp stone hem.

Josh wonders again why it feels like this is the only

alternative to giving himself to the cold water and the speeding current of the river where it runs fast and churns itself blue-black, rushing towards the freedom of the sea. He laughs and clears his throat and she laughs too, and when he looks across at her there's something in her eyes that makes his heart speed up and palpitate and he thinks he might die anyway, right here in this dingy, mouldy flat in this huge mad city that he's lost himself in, ever since he stormed away from his mother and his grandmother and his tiny walled-in life. Come on, Josh, she's saying. Come on, please, tell me the story. And she sounds like she truly wants to hear it, or maybe she's a really good liar, but he thinks of the flooding river, and how she'd made him step backwards from it, and he restarts.

He went on the road when his mother had her seventh child. He wasn't banished, but he knew the burden he was. A blind child was no use except as a beggar, and he couldn't be a beggar in his own village. A year after a fever had taken his sight his father had made him a kind of a glove from the hard wood of a carob tree, hardened further with some acrid potion made from the mulched flower and gum of a cypress. The glove was of two separate parts, one fitting over his thumb and the other fitting over his four fingers. His father showed him how to use the device to see. The echo of the sound it made when the thumb piece was clacked against the finger piece would tell him the size and shape and texture of an object in his path, and soon he was able to make out trees and walls and the sides of paths, and the holes opened in them by rain, and discarded pots and rocks and stones of nearly every size, and he learnt to walk without stumbling, without even using the thin straight stick his father had carved for him from an oak branch to feel his way.

And so the day he left he took with him his wooden clacking glove and his father's old staff, fractured from some encounter with a recalcitrant beast and fastened with gut wire, just strong enough to aid his walking, and the patched robe and rough cloak he always wore. He left in the early morning and he crested the slope of their valley at noon. He felt the sun directly above him as it passed through its hottest meridian. He knew the scents of early spring, of sap rising and flowers opening their hearts to bees, of the enriching sullage of animals spread along the furrows of turned earth. He knew the calls of birds but not their names, so he amused himself and diverted his thoughts from his mother and father and his brothers and sisters by naming the birds he heard singing, using the sound peculiar to each species to form a name for it, and it occurred to him that each species would have a male and a female, and that they would likely have a different call and song, and so he tuned his ear to returned calls, to answers given in trills or tunes, and he presumed the singers of long, involved songs, the show-offs, the implorers, to be males, and the perfunctory, sweetly trilling answerers to be female.

Josh finds himself forgetting to breathe, letting the words struggle from him in a rush above a held breath. He feels embarrassed suddenly and the feeling becomes exquisite, unbearable. Jesus. The words he'd used, the way he'd written it. *Recalcitrant? Sullage? Perfunctory?* What had he been thinking? Why had he written the story in such a heightened, false voice? He feels his embarrassment heating and reddening his face and neck and ears, sweat breaking through his skin: he feels like vomiting.

Honey shifts one leg up under her and Josh can see the bone of her ankle beneath the hem of her jeans, above her Converse. He imagines himself kissing that sharpness softly, then kissing behind her knee, and up along her to her hands and then her neck and lips. She has a distant expression and the ghost of a smile on her lips and she sighs again and says, Oh, Josh. You're so funny when you read. So serious. And the way you say the words so carefully. Like they're the most important words in the world.

His embarrassment cedes ground to anger in a few pounding heartbeats and he closes his hand around the pages he's read so that they bunch and nearly tear and she says, Jesus, what are you doing? Don't tear your lovely story! Josh, are you okay? He remembers then why this story means so much, and he feels his shame and anger retreat a little, enough so that he's able to tell her that the story was his father's idea, that they'd been to Mass together one Saturday evening, just the two of them, that his father loved going to Mass though he wasn't even really a Catholic, that he really listened to the gospel stories because they reminded him of his parents, who knew the gospels forward and back and could quote whole passages word for word. How his father had talked all the way down the hill to the village and back up the hill from the main road to the cottage about the blind man in the Gospel of John. About how the blind man must have felt, being questioned by the Pharisees about Jesus, and by Jesus's disciples about his mother and his father, and how it must have felt to see, having been blind for so long. I tell you, Joshy, we ain't getting the full story from old Gospel-writing John. He's holding out on us bad!

Honey is sitting now on the edge of the couch, leaning towards him, and she's watching his eyes. Mothers and fathers. God, God, the pain they cause, when they're meant to stand between their child and pain, meant to soak it, stem it, stop it, kiss it better. She tells him how her mother had turned from the back of her boyfriend's car, one hand on the rim of the open boot lid, and mouthed something at her, something that looked like the shape of *I'll miss you* but she wasn't sure: her lips had met in a way they wouldn't have for *I love you*, to say *I love you* lips don't need to meet, but *miss* requires a meeting of the lips, *miss miss miss*, *love love love*, see the difference? But you can change memories to suit yourself, to fit across the shapes of your wounds, and if she asked her mother now what she had said her mother would say that she'd said, I love you, if that was what she wanted to hear.

She tells Josh how her father had stood silently in the doorway, watching her mother leave. How silent he'd been, how still. She couldn't understand how her mother could all of a sudden not love him. How anyone could not love him. Even in his madness he was perfect. Even the worst of him was perfect, was as he was meant to be.

Josh doesn't answer, just looks at her, then down at his pages, and he reads on.

WOULD THEY SEARCH *for him? he wondered. Would his father walk the fields and rises of the valley calling his name? Would he walk the river's banks or wade along it, trawling for his blind son's body? Would he stop where the river ran to marsh at the valley's flat mouth and look along the reeking plain before turning for home and his herds of small beasts and growing children, shrugging as he went? It didn't matter now. He held his left arm out and clacked, and knew the road ahead was straight, and that it would slope gently downwards for just shy of five miles, and that it would rise then steeply to a pass between two hills, and he knew that there was a small grove or copse of trees at the foot of the nearest hill, and that a small stream had cut a path from the hill's eastern face and that it wound down around the grove, and he knew when he came a little closer, clacking all the while, that there were fruit trees in the grove, and he knew from their smell that there were late olives and early mangoes and some other sharp-smelling, unripe fruit he didn't recognize, and that he'd have food and water and shelter when he felt the cooling of the day. And he was, unexpectedly, content.*

He walked clacking through the grove to find the tree with the thickest branches, with the heaviest canopy for his camp. He knew from the great height of the trees and their irregular branches and the thinness of the flesh of the olives in his mouth that they were wild trees, not cultivated by villagers or a farmer, who would prune the trees low and squat, and breed the fruit to fatness. He was further from his home than he had ever been, by a factor of twenty or so, he guessed. Further perhaps than even his father had ever been. He wondered if this meant that he was brave. He drank from the shallow stream, and its water was sweet and cool, and he ate sparingly, though he knew the fruit of the trees was good, and he knew it was wild, but still he felt a kind of guilt, as though he were a thief not used to stealing.

He slept that night beneath a tree whose trunk was forty paces around. He made his bed in a mossy cleft between the tops of two mighty roots, and he felt as he drifted to sleep the kindness of the tree, its knowing of his presence there, its pleasure at the warmth of him against its bark. No rabbits would come gnawing with this creature at its foot. The whitefly might be frightened of his smell. A low humming seemed to come from some place beneath the tree, to suffuse the boy, to soothe his aching body, his burning feet, and he slept deeply into the morning, and all he could remember of his dreams when he woke was that they were sweet.

OH, HONEY SAYS, in a soft voice, and Josh stops reading and looks up at her, and he realizes that the hand holding his pages is shaking a little. She's smiling at him, a kind of a sad smile but beautiful, and she smells so sweet he feels his head spin. He wonders again what he was thinking when he wrote this story, draft after draft of it in blue biro on lined A4 jotter pages, at the kitchen table in the cottage, at the small desk in his room, on the bus from Nenagh to Dublin and on the ferry across to Wales and the bus from there to London, in the squat where he'd lived for a while, and now in this tiny wet-walled flat. How important it seemed as he was writing it, how ridiculous it seems now, how alien, how forced and contrived and show-off-y, all the big words and the ridiculous tone and the rubbish about the clacker and the trees. But all that stuff was true, he knew, about clackers being used for navigation by blind people, and trees humming with life, drawing power up from the soil, from the flesh of the earth. Fuck it. He might as well read on.

HE WALKED LIKE this until the days he'd spent walking equalled the years he'd been alive. So half a month had passed before he stopped, at the edge of a town. He held himself straight and still before he approached the town's gates, taking the air of the place, feeling against his skin the winds of it, tasting its scents. He knew he'd walked away from the sea but still he tasted salt in the breeze, and spices and perfumes and a milling stink, and he guessed that this was a place of traders, of resting caravans and lousy burdened beasts, where people bartered to live and alchemized found things to ore. He kept his left hand inside his cloak and clacked softly so as to avoid attention, straining to receive the echoes so he might plot his path through the bazaars and spidering streets, and find a place to sit and be a beggar. Trees gave easily, and cared only that you twisted their bounty gently from the branch. People, he knew, would hold faster to their fruit.

He found a shaded place against a low wall flanked by a row of cypress trees. No one yelled at him to move and he removed his cloak and folded it by his feet and laid his cracked staff at his side and waited, and some alms were left on his cloak and he thanked the almsgivers softly, and some asked him where he was from, and he told them the name of his village, and a woman said she knew the place, she'd been there once for a wedding, and the people of that place were kind. And her voice had a trill to it, like an answering bird, and he found that his voice when he replied to her had the susurrations and imploring tone of a cocking male, and he wondered at himself, at the warmth rising inside him, at the pounding just then started in his chest. Come to my house, she said, and have your evening meal. You're just a boy and far from home, and you must have walked with God to have come this far alone and be unharmed.

She danced for him that evening for the first time. And every evening after that he walked the streets from his begging spot by the line of cypresses in the shady square to her house and she gave him his evening meal and danced. And he clacked his thumb piece on her table-top in time with the gentle beat of her feet on the packed earth of the floor of her house. And to watch her dance he needed no clacker, just to sit still, without even drawing breath, and to feel the eddies and vortices of her, the breezes and winds she made with her body, the sweet gentle zephyrs of perfume and sweat. She hummed softly as she danced, and she sang sometimes in a language he'd never heard, but a word here and there of her song would seem familiar, but the meaning of the words would evanesce before his understanding, like dreams before memory. He always knew when it was time to go. She'd stop dancing and be silent and he'd take his leave without a word. And after a while men began to press gold pieces into his palm and ask in low voices whether the woman was in her house and whether she was receiving visitors that day, and he would lead them to her door and tap with his staff, and sometimes she would open the door and thank him, and the man would press past him into the house and the door would close and he'd go back to his begging spot, and sometimes she would say, No, and the man behind him would sigh and whine and remonstrate with him as though it were his fault, and always those times he would give back the gold piece.

And every night he slept in a small wood on the side of a low hill near the town's perimeter, but on the far side from the town so that the sun set later and rose earlier on him, and the tree he slept beneath was of similar girth and height to the one he'd slept beneath on the first night of his journey, and its branches were thick and close and they hung low above him, so that their fronds sometimes stroked him as he slept, and his bed was in a mossy cleft between two roots just as it had been on the first night. And his alms were always plenty so he rarely knew hunger or thirst and he gave the greater portion of his coins to the woman and the rest he gave to other beggars. And children sometimes followed him to his tree, but they never teased him the way they teased the other crippled beggars, just asked him how it was that he could see with his eyes closed, and they'd ask him if they could see his eyes, and he'd open them, though to do so caused him pain, and they'd gasp in wonder at the blueness of his eyes, at the useless rolling orbs at their centre, and they'd play a game where they'd hold an object up before him, a water jar, say, or the branch of a tree, or a loaf of bread, and he'd clack his wooden glove and guess, always correctly, what the object was, and the children would squeal in terror and delight at this magic. They'd ask if they could wear his strange glove and he'd let them, and he'd let his softened fingers take the sun while they played at being the blind clacking beggar, and he'd bite his nails down to the quick.

Before he slept each night, even when the wind blew cold from the north, he felt a warmth flow upwards into him from the earth. He felt a vibration as tiny and as fast as the heartbeat of an insect from the wood of the tree, through its rough bark, through the *exposed tops of the roots that fortressed him. He felt the fingers and thumb of his left hand joining with the wood from the carob tree from which his father had made his clacking glove and he felt the glove joining with the wood of the tree, its hardened resin mixing with the fresh resin on the living bark, and he felt the tree extend its roots and lift its crown and whisper to the trees around it, asking if they needed help, if they knew of any trees that needed help, and the trees' whispers spread like his imagining of the ripples of a pebble in a pond, out and out and out across the land to other lands and to the sea, crossing with an infinity of other rippling whispers, and he felt the moon and the winking stars and their heavenly accordance, their shared intent, their knowing of each other and of him, and he knew this world was not the only world, that this was not the centre or the stage, but only a tiny and equally weighted part of an unimaginable whole, and he felt the speed of spinning as he slept, on the round belly of a giant.*

SLOWLY, JOSH, HONEY says. You need to appreciate your own words. You need to let each sentence have its space. Widen your vowel sounds. Josh feels a hot prickling on his forehead and cheeks and neck. He knows his voice is grating, stupid, countrified, barely intelligible to this smart, beautiful city girl, this streetwise strutting angel. Even the way she smokes is cool, the way her lips pucker slightly as she exhales in a long stream, and he tries to inhale her smoke so that what was inside her will be inside him. She changed into her waitress uniform in his room last night. A tight black skirt and white blouse. She left her Pixies T-shirt on his duvet. Gigantic, gigantic, my big, big love. He pressed it to his face as he lay unsleeping, inhaling her. She hasn't asked for it, she mustn't have noticed, or maybe she left it on purpose, a claim-flag, her territory staked.

THE SEASONS FOLDED over on each other one by one, and he was a man. And the woman still was waiting every night. And still he guided cocking birds to her door when he was asked, and sometimes their imploring calls were answered and sometimes not. And the winds of her were changed but no less beautiful; he was better able to measure them now and to know the exactness of her steps, and to know the length of her arms and legs and her fingers and to know the curve of her cheek and the shape and the plumpness of her lips, the gentle valley of her lower back, the perfect line along it, the heart-scalding press of her bones through her skin, the pucker above her lip, like a tiny riverbed, the drop of the lobes of her ears. She took his hand one evening and led him from the table and laid him down and lay beside him stretched full and pushed against him and she was naked and so was he and the shutters of her house were locked and for the first time that he could remember he wished to God that he could see.

Something had changed in the town the next day. He could hear from as far away as the brow of the hill, as he walked with his clacker and staff, an uncommon hubbub from the walls of the town, and the tramping of a column of people, like a cavalry unhorsed and unarmed, and people were shouting greetings from the walls to the newcomers, and others were shouting warnings and threats. He hesitated on the hill but curiosity drove him on.

143

He clacked and picked his way across the thronging crowd to his place at the line of cypress trees in the shady square, and he sat and listened and tasted the strange scent that hung above the market like a cloud. The newcomers weren't traders or farmers with produce to sell, or merchants or performers or officials sent from a city to take counts and extract taxes: they were the followers of a preacher who said he was from God. And almost as soon as he had deduced this he heard a shuffling at either side and in front of him and he was taken by the arms and legs and lifted up and carried away from his begging place. Some instinct told him not to shout or struggle and he knew that the men carrying him were strong: their breathing was unlaboured and their movements were sure and quick; they carried him as though he were a child.

They carried him along the streets and people shouted, Put him down! You have no right to take him like that! But he was just a beggar and no one, he knew, would block their path or try to free him from their grip. He wasn't used to travelling at this speed or at this angle, and he was overwhelmed by his fear, and so he lost his bearings. But he didn't dare clack to take a measure of his position even though his arms hung loose along the sides of the captors holding his top half. He curled his left hand closed so his half-glove was as good as fully hidden and he hoped they wouldn't notice it and take it from him. He imagined himself without it, groping with his staff, a cripple, a blind man. His staff! It would be gone when he returned, he knew, if he ever returned to his shady seat by the cypress trees, the throw of a stone from the house of his love.

JOSH, HONEY SAYS. I have to go now. I'm already late for my shift. But I'll be back tomorrow for the next part. Thinking about your story will get me through the evening, like a dream. No matter how rude the customers are I'll just take their orders with a smile and imagine the blind man, asleep and happy at the foot of his tree.

Josh is satisfied with this. The thought of his story being in her thoughts, meaning something to her, existing somewhere outside his own mind, outside these thin biro marks on A4 pages. The thought that she'll be back again, that she'll bus from Notting Hill up to here and walk from the stop to the door downstairs and press the buzzer for number three and say into the intercom, It's me.

THEY STILL HADN'T spoken by the time they put him down. He sat upright on the ground and folded his arms in front of himself and said, Where is my staff? It is my only possession besides my clothes. Don't worry, brother, one of them said, I have it. It's not much of a staff, though. It's held together with the gut string of a pig. And the spit of a whore, someone else said, and there was rowdy laughter from the assembly, and they sounded like two score at least. And more then joined them from downwind and he could smell their unwashed bodies and he could hear that there were four of them at least and he knew from the sudden hush and the pulse through the crowd that the leader of these people was among them.

He knew from the shifting wind that the leader was standing before him and he clacked to take the leader's measure without thinking and someone fell on him and seized him roughly by the arm and pulled from his fingers and his thumb the two parts of his wooden glove and said, What is this? Why do you aim this at the Messiah? And he heard himself laugh and he heard the splitting air beside his face before he felt the sting of someone's open hand across his cheek, and he fell sideways and something lightened and loosened inside him and his waters made a paste around him in the dust. And the leader spoke in a voice loud and even saying, Don't hurt him. Have you not listened to me all these days? My only command: hurt no one. Our task is to deliver, not to condemn, to save, not to destroy. And there was a low rumbling of voices, a ripple of mumbled contrition.

And then he felt the wind of the leader bending down, and this man who they said was a messiah rubbed a warm paste onto his eyelids, and he wondered if it was the paste of his own water and the dust of the ground, and the leader's touch was gentle but the blind man dared not resist or protest or even move his head. Leave this paste on your eyes for a day, the leader said. When you wash it away you will no longer be blind. You will not need this wooden glove to see. And the leader placed first the finger piece and then the thumb piece onto the blind man's hand and he embraced him in a strange way, with his hand on the blind man's forehead and his arm crooked around the blind man's head, and the leader kissed the blind man on the side of his face.

They told him they had made their camp at the town gates and that he was welcome to eat with them that night but he left, testing the ground ahead with the point of his staff before regaining his bearings with his clacker: the town walls in the distance and the opened gates, the communal olive grove at the bend of the road leading west, the hills in the distance, his own hill in the nearer distance, with his own grove on its far side and his kind, sheltering tree. Some of the followers of the magician or the Messiah or the preacher – he had heard him being called all these things in the course of that strange day – followed him a little way, exclaiming at his sure and steady step, asking had he been cured already, was their leader's power so strong, and he tried to explain how he listened to the quality of the echoes of the sound made by his clacker and that was how he distinguished the obstacles in his path, how he knew the lie of the land around him. But they wouldn't listen: they shouted and laughed and ran ahead of him and stood still in

147

his path to see if he would walk into them, and one of them tried to take the clacker from his hand and he closed his fist tight and the man stopped trying and walked, spitting, away. They left him then, shouting warnings back that he was to do as the Messiah said, to leave the blessed dirt on his eyes until the next day, and then to wash so he would see and he would know that he had met the true father, and he would worship him.

OH, GOD, HONEY says. This is all going to go wrong, isn't it? Poor blind man. I kind of love him. Is that weird? Josh shakes his head and smiles at her. How much is left? she asks. We're about halfway, he says. Oh, good, she says. I don't want it to end too soon. I want to get two more shifts out of it at least. The sound of your voice kind of buzzes round my head for hours after I leave here, and the blind man clacks around in there, and I think about him and he has your face.

Josh has three early shifts in a row and Honey has three late shifts, and he expects her on the fourth day but she doesn't come and he's afraid to leave the flat even to go to the shop for a few minutes in case she comes and rings the bell and leaves again, so he drinks the brackish London water from the rusty tap and eats the cereal and stale bread and hardening cuts of ham he stole from the kitchen and the small jars of preserves pilfered from the breakfast room, secreted in his backpack. He starts to think she's grown sick of him and he feels his spirit sagging, he feels a weight of loneliness he's never felt before, he feels he might even cry, and he wonders at this, how it could be possible.

He hardly cried when his father died, just lay still for days and didn't speak for weeks. His thoughts were all like clouds, random and shapeless and weightless, drifting. And when his granddad went he was the same, though not as obviously so; at the Mass he'd read a eulogy he'd written, and he was told over and over how lovely his words were, how he'd done poor Paddy proud. And he'd tried and tried to cry and he could not.

The bell rings and he runs to the window and sees the tight braids on the top of her lovely head and she's wearing a black T-shirt and light-coloured jeans and she seems to sense him there looking because she raises her face and sees him and smiles up at him and waves, and he thinks he could happily live this single moment for infinity, that no moment could be as perfect and beautiful as this moment, this beautiful creature on the fouled pavement under the dank sky outside his crumbling building, smiling up at him, looking at him through her brown eyes, her deep brown eyes, her beautiful, beautiful eyes.

Spare the story, she says. I don't want the reading of it to be over. Tell me something about you. And he thinks maybe he should reverse this, ask her to tell him about herself, that maybe he'll look like a self-absorbed arsehole if he allows her again to draw him out, and he rabbits on and on about his childhood and his mother and father and how his paradise turned dark, and maybe she has greater sorrows in her life than he, and thinks him stupid and narcissistic and selfish, but listens to him out of some altruistic impulse, some fear, based on the miserableness of his aspect and his surroundings and his self-imposed exile, the big stupid sulk that led him here to this alien place where his father was born, that he might throw himself into the river or under a bus, or because maybe she has nothing better to do between the time her bus drops her on Clerkenwell Road and the start of her shift except listen to his juvenile bullshit.

For all his doubts he starts to speak, and he tells her about the day his father died. He remembers the way the breeze

150

stopped blowing and the birds stopped singing when he looked from the orchard to the halfway gate and saw a policeman opening it, and heard his mother saying, That's Jim Gildea, oh, sweet Jesus, what does he want? And Ellen Jackman standing and his grandmother standing, saying, Lord Jesus, what now? He remembers the expression on Jim Gildea's face, and the slow way he took off his hat as he approached them and how he couldn't hear what the policeman was saying because there was a whooshing sound in his ears but it was something about him because everyone was turning to look at him, and Ellen Jackman was taking his hand and they were walking together into the house and he could see from the half-door his mother with her hands over her face and his grandmother with one hand over her mouth as if to stop herself saying something, and his grandfather was coming now, up the lane on his bicycle, and his hair was floating out behind him the way it always did, and he was dropping his bicycle by the yard gate and he was walking with his hands out towards his daughter and his wife and the young policeman with the red face.

He tells her about the way his grandfather told him what had happened, kneeling beside him, talking to him like he was a baby even though he was twelve, nearly thirteen, nearly a man, saying, Your daddy had an accident, on the road, someone hit him by accident when he was unloading a trailer, he wouldn't have known a thing about it, and he's up in Heaven now, so he is, because your father never sinned as long as I've known him and I doubt he ever sinned his whole life long, and there's a special place in Heaven for people like your daddy, and we won't see him again in this life, so we won't, but he'll be with us always, and some day we'll see him again.

HE DIDN'T EAT that night in the woman's house, and nor did he feel hungry. He wondered if she'd dance anyway, without him there to keep time for her with his tapping clacker; he wondered if she'd walk out into the street and along it to the square to search for him. A misting rain fell on his hill and he was careful to stay in the shelter of his tree, in the crook of its roots, for fear that the rain would wash the crusted paste from his eyes and the newcomers would find him and accuse him of disobeying their leader and punish him. He lay curled close to the tree's trunk and at some point in that night he slept and he dreamt of a light coming towards him, of perfect uncorrupted white, but he woke before it could reach him and envelop him and . . . and he found when he woke that his face was wet and at first he thought that he'd been crying in his sleep, but he realized that he was wet through, that the rain had worked its way through the branches and leaves of his tree, and he rubbed his eyes and found that the paste was nearly gone, washed by the insinuating rain, and the last of it came away in the fingers of his right hand, and his eyes opened as if of their own accord and he turned his face to the world outside his hiding place and he saw that the rain had formed small streams in the hollows between the roots of trees all around the grove, and they ran in narrow tributaries to the river in the valley below, and he looked a long while at these new streams, and he thought how they made it seem as though the hill itself were crying, and he touched the fingers of his right hand again to the lids of his eyes and he wondered how a dream could feel so real, how a man who was sleeping could feel so awake.

He couldn't shake himself out of the dream and so he decided to move through it, and to enjoy the sensation of being in a dream and being aware of it, a thing that happened now and then but rarely, and never for as long as this. He walked down the weeping hill to the ford of the river and across it to the town's gates and his eyes were stung by the light, but they soon became adjusted to being opened. It was early in the morning and so the gates were closed and the sentry was sleeping in his box on the small lookout tower above the entrance. The blind man stood and waited and the sentry stirred, as though he'd sensed his presence there. He grunted and spat and descended his tower, and the blind man heard him at the far side of the gate, drawing back the heavy bolt. The sentry was short and squat and his red bulbous face was covered with boils and the blind man found himself laughing at the sight of him, and the sentry asked, What's funny, stranger? And the blind man wondered why this man who saw him every day would call him stranger.

He moved along his dream world through the streets, and he wondered at their colourlessness, the dank unremitting greyness of the ground and the buildings, as though the rain had caused the houses and shops to sprout overnight from the earth, like strange angular flowers. And his clacker felt heavy on his hand and he tested it against the walls around him, and its echoed sounds were jumbled and indistinct, damped by the rain, perhaps, and even with his eyes closed he couldn't map the town, and everything was where it should have been but nothing looked as he thought it should, and he hoped he'd wake soon from this strange, lifeless dream. He found his begging place, and the cypresses that sentried it were not straight and noble and rich green as he had imagined: they were crooked and sparse and sickly and two or three were a burnt brown colour, as though they'd died and withered in the sun. He laid his cloak folded as he always did and he laid his poor staff on top of it and he sat and closed his eyes and prayed to God that he would wake soon and be blind.

JOSH FINDS HIMSELF now preparing things to tell Honey about himself. She seems to need to hear about the things that had happened to him, and as he tells her about them they take on a kind of lightness: they seem to lift themselves up from the clay and grass and narrow tarmac road and glinting lake-water and whispering trees of his home and curl and twirl, like smoke, upwards, outwards, towards nowhere.

He lets himself drift backwards in time and he watches scenes from his past as an impassive observer, like someone watching a film they've seen a dozen times before. Andrew Jackman and two of his friends from college or the city, or wherever Andrew Jackman was when he wasn't at home, all on horseback on the lane, high horses and dark, snorting steam from their nostrils. Blocking the path so he can't pass either side of them, and the horses frighten him a bit because they're stepping sideways and forward and back and so he presses himself close to the wall and waits. Is that him? one of Andrew's friends is asking. Yes, Andrew answers, smiling strangely, look-ing not at Joshua but up the lane towards the cottage and the hilltop behind it. Well, he doesn't look one bit black. Except for his hair and lips, maybe a tiny bit. His father is properly black? Like, black-black? Not half-caste or anything? As black as night, Andrew answers. You might see him later if my dad has him working for us today. That's fucking amazing, the friend says. And they kick their heels into their horses' ribs and trot away from him, up the lane, and he thinks about lying down on the ground in the high grass beneath the alder by the stream and waiting there for his father to come and find him, and he'll tell him what Andrew Jackman and his friends said and how they made him feel, and his father will laugh and say, Don't worry, Little Bud-oh, they're just jealous of you. But he never did. He never told anyone what happened on the lane that day.

Honey now has a tear in her eye and he thinks he's over-done it, that he's pushed this thing too far, tried to wring too much from it. She'll see him now as a victim, a cowed little child, someone to be pitied and protected, not someone who could be her protector, her man, her lover. Oh, Josh, she's say-ing, and it feels like a thousand times at least she's said it, and her pity is starting to worry him. He's frightened he'll blow his chance with her by being pathetic. Will I read the next bit? he says, and he tries to say it in a manly way, and she laughs and looks a bit puzzled, but she sits back in the way she always does, with one leg tucked beneath her, and today she's wearing a lower top than usual, and a colourful billowy skirt, and her hands are folded on her lap, and he wants to lie over there along the couch with his head on her lap so she can stroke his hair and whisper to him that she loves him, that he's her man, that everything now is going to be okay.

AND AFTER A while he came to know that he was awake, that the promised miracle had been delivered and that the sight of his eyes had been returned to him. He didn't stir, just sat and watched the shadows grow along the ground with the arcing movement of the sun, afraid to look up at the strange world. None of the passers-by seemed familiar and none were almsgivers because it was the day after the Sabbath and that was the leanest day of all for beggars. Eventually he heard a voice and he knew it was one of his fellow beggars, a crippled man who hobbled on a crutch. Hey, you, he said. Why are you sitting in my friend's place and wearing his clothes? Where is my friend the blind man? And the blind man said, Friend, it is me. I was cured yesterday by the leader of the newcomers, the one they say is the Messiah. But his friend would not believe him and he steadied himself against the low wall so that he could strike the blind man's legs with his crutch, and the blind man held up his left hand and said, See, it is me, here is my glove, but the cripple would not believe him. Others came, beggars mostly, and some believed him and fell on the ground before him, and more called him a liar and a thief, and someone picked his staff up from his folded cloak and smashed it against the edge of the wall.

He stood and pushed through the small braying mob and fled along the narrow streets towards the woman's house. He closed his eyes, though even the darkness now was unfamiliar but he let his legs carry him and his left hand work at the clacker, watching for obstacles in his path, but there were none. At the door of the woman's house he stopped and opened his eyes, and he saw that the door was damaged: the wood of it had been struck and splintered, and it opened slowly before him and a hag stood there looking out, toothless and drooped and ancient, lined like a sundried windfall, with long clawed hands that she held linked before her as though they pained her, and when she spoke he knew this was the woman who had fed him and danced for him and to whom he had given his love and a daily handful of coins, and he felt as though he had been tricked, that this was a witch who had cast a spell on him, and only the weakest of spells was needed, he knew, to bewitch a man who saw with his ears and heard with his hand. Who are you? she asked, and he closed his eyes against the truth of her and turned away and walked back to his begging place, slowly, shielding his eyes against the alien sun.

SHIFTS AT THE café are bearable when they wind slowly down towards evenings and nights that will be spent with him. With the angles and shots and scenes of him, his face and voice and lilting story, his blind man shuffling towards danger. She hasn't spent the night yet. She wants to but she's not sure how to broach it. She has to get to the inside of him. He's asking her to lead him somewhere, and his hands shake and his voice trembles as he reads to her and she still can't quell the rising urge to laugh at him, at his little bundle of paper, his scrunched serious face, the way he bends over his words and lets his voice fade to a whisper at the end of each paragraph. There's no point trying to be cool around him, no point in acting, or holding back.

Is this how you know you're in love? This absence of pretence? She'd thought for a little while that she was in love with her tutor in college. Good-looking, she supposed, though studiedly unkempt. Leaning over her workstation, pretending to be interested, always pretending. The sweaty nutty musk of him, the deathly sweetness of his breath. Saying, That's really good, Honey. Leaving his hand too long on her shoulder, the tip of a finger resting on her bra strap, pulsing there. Offering to take her out. To show her his collection of French *noir*. To loan her his vintage cine camera, his '52 Paillard Bolex, though

159

he'd have to give her a pretty intense crash course on how to use it properly. She saw the truth of him pretty quickly, felt the tremble in the air around his lie about being separated from his wife, only sharing the house still because rent was so high. She started to hate when he spoke to her, always from above her, it seemed. Why were men always hulking, folding themselves down from above, eyes flashing with some feverish light that never seemed to dull, their teeth in those moments always seeming jagged, shaped to rip flesh from bone? The shapes men take for the hunt, contorting themselves into some ancient template, cloaking themselves against their savage truths.

Her ex, Saul, huge and lean, arching himself downwards towards her, something flashing always in his eyes, some furious crazy mix of excitement and anger, reproach and apology; Saul was always close to madness. He screamed when she told him it was over, high-pitched, trembling at the end, disbelief in his eyes, like a child who's fallen and has discovered that they're bleeding, that their life is seeping from inside them, the shocking wet redness of their pain. He swung his open hand at her face and she ducked and parried, like her dad had taught her, like his dad had taught him, and then she'd turned and run. He came to the caff a couple of times and stood at the counter staring, and she'd hissed at him to piss off and he had. She knew he was scared of her father. What kind of cold, scary world do girls live in who haven't been blessed with dangerous, loving fathers?

She should be bored of this by now. Listening. Josh is looking at her from across the small room through the blue haze of her cigarette smoke, worry in his eyes, or guilt, contrition. Is this his act? This pretence at innocence, at vulnerability, this pale scraggly aspect he assumes, this malnourished existence? He bathes in sadness, it seems, lets it wash over him and into him and out of him. This story he's written, and the poem she picked up from the floor, his attempt to corral it, to tame it from wildness so it won't kill him. Or maybe just to know where it is so it can't blindside him, attack him, claws drawn, from behind. Or maybe this is his cloak, this sublimation, his hunter's camouflage, his hidden jaggedness. Or maybe he's different. Her stomach tells her that he is, her lack of nausea, of prickling distant fear. The way his voice washes softly against her. The way he seems to want to listen when she speaks.

She tells Josh something she's never told anyone. About her dad, how he hated loud noise. How he would shrink from it, hands on ears, eyes tight closed, then, failing to cease it, attacking it with his fists. One Sunday morning he smashed a boom box on the street outside their house. His church trousers on, his feet bare, his shirt open, he rushed through the door and grabbed it from a guy's shoulder and threw it on the pavement so hard that bits of it flew across the street and landed in the high grass at the edge of the park. He told the guy he'd do him next and the guy called him a fucking psycho, but not until he was at a safe distance. He punched a man through the open window of a car once. When she was nine or maybe ten, but only barely, and had been walking with him to the shop. The man had been shouting into a handheld mouthpiece, his tinny voice amplified by a plastic trumpet on the car's roof. VOTE CONSERVATIVE was printed in high white letters on the car's slab sides. Your Conservative candidate, the man had been saying, and then the start of the candidate's name, Sir something. Her father, still holding her hand, had reached a long arm out from the kerb as the car crawled past and the man's eyes had filled with fear and his mouth was diverted from the candidate's name to an O of shock as his head half turned to meet Syd Bartlett's fist.

And she'd laughed. It seemed so comical, the way it had all happened so suddenly, so smoothly, the way the man's fortunes had changed so completely in an instant, the way his hand was still up in front of his face, empty now, the way his car was still rolling. The open-mouthed, bloodied silence of the man, still moving at the same speed, like a cartoon cat sliced in two by a cartoon mouse, like Wile E. Coyote running on thin air, not yet realizing he's run out of solid ground. Her father saying, Fuck you and your Tory bastard candidate. He didn't fight no fucking war. Even now it seems funny, though she'd cried for hours that night as her father hid in a neighbour's attic, and seven men from their street were taken to a police station to stand in an identity parade, even the man whose house her father had taken refuge in. Her father said his fear of noise came from a place called Goose Green, when he was in 2 Para. In a war over an island far away, down near the bottom of the world. She remembered his absence, her mother's friends calling, the house full of smoke and low voices. She was ashamed of the fact that she didn't know more.

Her father hated her mother's noise most of all. He'd sit still when she started to shout, then cup his hands over his mouth and nose after a while, and she thinks now looking back that he was re-inhaling his own breath, using his own carbon dioxide to calm himself, the way someone hyperventilating would blow into and suck a paper bag. On TV at least. It never worked for her dad. He always stood eventually, knocking his chair backwards, advancing towards her mother with his great fists raised, and he'd always swing but he'd never connect; the swinging and missing was a way it seemed of shocking his wife into silence, into stillness, and she'd always say something like, Go on, then. Go on, then, big man. Hit me. Hit me. I dare you. But always in a low voice, a breathless whisper, and her father would squeeze his eyes closed, like he was in pain, and Honey was always shocked at the sight of her father's tears, and her mother's, and she wondered always why they couldn't just love each other quietly, fervently, the way she loved both of them.

THE PHARISEES' MEN *came next to torment him. He was dragged bodily away again, as he sat cradling his broken staff, mourning it, the work of his father's kind old hands. He closed his left fist tight to protect his clacker, and he tried and tried to keep his feet as they dragged him, and he told them there was no need to man-handle him, that he would walk with them to wherever it was they wanted him to go. But they wouldn't listen and they held his arms high behind him to the point of breaking them, and he cried from the pain and the salt of his tears burnt his eyes. Some of the voices around him he knew: some were of other beggars who were shouting that he was a liar and a thief; some were of almsgivers who were saying that this was not the blind man, that this was an imposter, one of the newcomers, the blasphemers who worshipped a false god, playing a trick to convince them that a miracle had been done. The blind man was thrown on the ground before the temple and someone placed their foot on his back so that he couldn't raise himself, and the sun had dried the ground again to dust and the dust filled his mouth and nose so that he could hardly breathe and all he could see was the Pharisees' leathered feet as they stood in a semi-circle before him. Who are you? they asked. I am the blind man from the square of cypress trees. I have begged there for three summers. Are you still blind? they asked. No, he said, now I can see. How did this come to be? they asked. The leader of the newcomers, the one they say is the Messiah – and here the foot was lifted from his back and used to kick him hard in the side so that his breath left him and he struggled to begin again to speak – rubbed a paste onto my eyes and told me to wait until morning and to wash the paste away and my sight would be restored. So this man who says he is from God performed this healing work on the Sabbath day? Yes, the blind man said, and he closed his eyes against his tears and the sight of their mobbing feet and the grey, dusty world.*

HONEY THINKS IT's funny how you sometimes, most times, have to be surprised into awareness of the strength of your own feelings. Ambushed by the truth of things. By a story Josh told her about a chambermaid in his hotel. Visiting him in the pot-wash during her quiet time, while she's waiting for her floor to empty out. Telling him how bored she is. Asking him all about himself. What? What did he fucking tell her? How many girls is he spilling his guts to? The chambermaid showed him a tattoo she got of a rose, right at the top of her leg. She had to hitch her black skirt up to show him. WHAT? Honey begs herself to keep calm, to stay contained, to say nothing. Inside her head she's screaming at the little bitch, Keep your skanky tattooed fanny away from my man. My man. Oh, the laugh. He's no man, this pale skinny refugee, this brown-eyed flotsam.

She closes her lips tight and breathes slowly in and out through her nose. She holds herself in place. She watches herself rising from the armchair and crossing the dingy timeworn rug and grabbing the pages from his hands, hears herself telling him to go fuck himself if he thinks she's gonna take three extra buses every night to sit here listening to his SHIT and she sees the pages tearing in her hands and she wonders how this will look, midway through, maybe, a narrative crux, panning slowly to his face and out of the window and up and up,

166

no, they'd never manage that with a hand-held, and she hears herself say, Sorry, shit, sorry, and his cheeks are snow white and his eyes are wet and wide with shock and he's saying, It's all right, I'll stick it back together, and she wants to put her arms around him and not let go until this feeling passes, of being beside herself, of him being beside himself, not able to pull themselves together, past all this sadness, this stupid love.

On the landing outside his flat, in the dim rising light from the open doorway below, in a soft bath of street sounds, engines and footfalls and voices and birdsong, she takes his right hand in her left and squeezes it and puts a hand on his shoulder to steady herself as she raises herself on tiptoe to kiss him on the lips, and he starts a little, as if surprised that this should happen, and she wonders if she's made a mistake, if she's misread his looks and his stumbling, mumbled attentiveness, his red-faced smiles. He's so different from the boys she knows, Saul, all the other Sauls that came before; he has none of their brim or swagger or braggadocio, none of their raw, seething desperation to undress her, pin her, press themselves against her. She wonders if he's gay. She decides that he's not. His free hand has moved to the back of her head and he's pressing her gently towards him and his lips are dry and sweet and she wonders again if, for the first time, she's actually in love.

H E WALKED FROM the town when the sun was high and unrelenting and his shadow was short. He had no staff, he had no cloak. His clacker still was safe in his clenched left hand. He thought for the first time about using it as a weapon if he was seized again, about lashing out with it, about resisting these people who vied for his truth. He crossed the ford and started up his hill, and the hill seemed smaller than it had been in his imagination, and to be scuffed with scrub and thorny bushes; the path he'd always taken seemed narrower than in his mind, and threatened more along its edges by nettles. He crested the hill and his heart settled a little at the sight of his tree: it was as wide and as high as he had measured with his hand and ear, and seemed to stand as steadfast on the slope as he had thought, pressing downwards and outwards with its roots, the ancient ruptures they had made ivied and mossed a dark welcoming green. But as he drew closer he noticed that the leaves of the tree and the wood of its branches were speckled white and the specks seemed to be moving and he thought to close his eyes fast against this new dawning truth but he was drawn forward and down, towards his dear tree, and he saw that its crown was a hazy diadem of whitefly and that their maggots had infested all its branches and its leaves and that the tree was dying, and he closed his eyes and listened, and he heard that its whispers were not offers of help but implorations, that the tree was a beggar like him.

He stumbled down the sunlit side and back across the ford and saw coming towards him the followers of the one they called Messiah and they were hooting and cheering as they approached and he saw that some of them were lame and some diseased and he wondered why their leader hadn't cured them, why he had seen fit instead to reserve his miracles for a beggar not known to him, and they were suddenly around him and they were lifting him and again, again, for the third time he was dragged and carried bodily away, and he closed his eyes again because he did not want to see.

They set him down before their leader and their leader asked him, Do you see? The blind man answered that he did. The followers whooped and cheered and proclaimed and some fell to their knees and their eyes rolled in their heads as though in a kind of reverie. The leader ignored them: his gaze was fixed on the blind man who now could see, and he asked, Do you believe I am the Son of God? This confused the blind man, and he was frightened and weary, and anger rose within him, like lava through a fissure in the earth, and he spat on the ground, and he said: I didn't ask for this, now let me be. And he was hurled to the ground again and blows were rained on him and the leader was shouting now, Stop this, don't hurt him, don't hurt him, but they kept on hitting him, and he lashed out with his left hand and it connected cleanly with someone's skull and the finger piece of his clacker split in two and fell from his hand, and he gave up then and lay still and accepted their blows.

As he slipped back to darkness the blows stopped and a new commotion started somewhere nearby. He heard the voices of the Pharisees and some of the townspeople and he saw from the ground that they were ranged across the roadway on one side of him and he turned his head and saw that the one they called Messiah and *his followers were ranged across the roadway on the other side of him. He saw that their Messiah was still, and that he seemed sad, and that his eyes were cast down, and that he didn't stand proud of his followers but in the middle of them. The blind man could see that the Messiah seemed to be overwhelmed by his followers, and to have lost all his authority, and that he alone was silent while the two groups traded insults and threats. The blind man felt a pain behind his eyes and a dimming of the light in them and he knew at once that his sight was leaving him again and he saw that the dust of the road around him was dark with his blood, and his blood was pooling outwards, and he felt that he was dying and was glad.*

THE LAST OF it then. The last part. A story about a house on a hill filled with love and a boy and his grandparents and his parents all crammed into it and the boy and his father driving out along a lake road and a trailer behind the car full of trees to be planted and the boy's father singing a song about birds, and singing a song about a man down a mine dying to save his friends, and the father sprinting in from midfield at full tilt and the crowd roaring on their hero and the net of the goal shaking and the father stopping suddenly and falling backwards and lying still and getting up from the ground, like a beautiful smiling Lazarus, and the boy and his father walking up from the village with their ice-cream cones.

But that all seems now like a dream, one of those dreams that feels when you wake from it like a whole life, every detail pristine and cutting-sharp until you think too much about them and they blur and fade and leave only a vague sense of themselves. A boy so loved he thinks the world is love without end. Grandparents, parents, in a circle around him adoring him. A boy walking with his friends across fields to the hurling pitch in Kilcolman, laughing. A boy with a dead father, his world turned cold and dark. A boy filled with rage, running, from a house of widows. Sailing on a ferry, bussing across Wales and England, thinking as the sun rises that all places are the same. Hills and rivers, roads and fields of grass. Walking out of Victoria coach station into a grey-brown thronged place. Labouring, washing dishes, living first in a squat and then in a dingy, death-scented flat. Thinking one morning: This is my last morning. Meeting a girl by the river that night and falling back from death and falling, falling.

And the Friday picnics in the summer and the excitement of waiting for his grandfather and his father to appear on the lane. And his father coming home for the last time and being lifted gently by six neighbours and friends and shouldered up the boreen from the hearse to the house and lying in the centre of the cottage, and the village all around him in a slowly moving ring, tearful and sorry. And Andrew Jackman and his friends looking down at him from their horses, talking about his father, whistling their amazement at his whiteness. The shame he'd felt at finding out, at thirteen years old, that Andrew Jackman's father owned the cottage and the orchard and the lane and the stile and the alder tree and all the oaks and the hillside and the stream and the bed he slept in. That his father, for all his work and all his goodness and all his plans, had died poor, owning nothing. The shame he felt for feeling such shame.

All the pain he'd caused his mother and his grandmother and his grandfather, getting into trouble in town, getting into fights, getting caught with an eighth of hash and being brought home by Jim Gildea who said, Sorry, Paddy. I had no choice. We had to charge him this time. But he'll probably only get a slap on the wrist. And his grandfather saying, Jesus Christ. Drugs. I never thought you'd do that to me, son, or to your mother or your grandmother or to your dear father. What must he be thinking, looking down at you?

The shame he'd felt at his grandfather's easy forgiveness. When he'd presented him on his seventeenth birthday with a white envelope containing a card, and in the card a voucher. For a week-long writing course. In Limerick. With a professional writer. The way you can hone your craft. Isn't that the way 'tis said? And his eyes stung and a lump like stone sat in his throat at the thought of his grandparents looking at the *Yellow Pages* and bussing it into Limerick and finding the place and asking for the voucher and talking to someone who might as well have been a Martian to them about how much it'd cost and what their grandson would get from his birthday present.

The shame he'd felt the day of Granddad's funeral that he'd come to nothing. Nineteen years old and no job, not enough points for college, fails in maths and science, his only good grade an A in English, and nothing to show for his talent there but a few half-arsed stories scribbled into a copybook. The dim hope he'd felt as the ferry had entered open water, that a storm might rise, that he might be thrown from the deck into the boundless sea.

And all these things tumbling around and knocking against each other, like stones on the bed of a rushing stream, their edges being lost in the attrition, worn to smoothness in the tumult, so that all he's left with is a single impression of a green and distant place filled with sorrow, with someone else's sadness and regret. He looks across at Honey, and she smiles, and he knows now how selfish he's been, how fixated on himself, but it's too late to stop now, too near the end, so he reads on, slowly, in a voice barely above a whisper.

THE NEWCOMERS AND the Pharisees fell silent and they looked as one to the west where a bright light was suddenly shining, of brilliant uncorrupted white. The light was moving along the road towards them, and they saw that it was a carter who was coming along the road, and his cart was drawn by oxen, and he was standing on the footboard of his cart and he had a tall staff in his right hand and a long silvered beard and he wore the thick coarse robe of a farmer and the sun had been reflecting off the clean whiteness of it and that was the moving light they had seen. The farmer drew his oxen to a stop and he descended the footboard and the newcomers parted to let him pass and he walked towards the bleeding man on the ground and he was saying, I heard a story from a traveller of a man who could see with his hand and his ear and I knew that it was you they spoke of. My son, my son, I searched for you, and searched for you. And I find you bleeding here. Who did this to you? And the Pharisees and the townspeople shuffled backwards and hung their heads and some of them turned away and made slowly for the town, and the followers of the Messiah turned their faces from this tall strong father and his bleeding, blinded son, and the father knelt and lifted the son from the ground, and he embraced him to his chest, and he lifted his face to the blue sky and sent his thanks for his found child, for the miracle that had been done. And he lifted his son to the bed of his cart and he turned for the long road home.

HONEY IS BESIDE him now. There's something wrong with Josh. He can't breathe, he can't get air fast enough into his lungs, he's drowning. He's fallen forward from his seat onto his knees and his hands are covering both sides of his face and his story is lying on the floor in front of him and something strange is happening to it: it's raining on it, huge drops are falling on it and melting the thin paper, and Josh thinks there must be a hole in the roof but he can't look up to check and his forehead now is almost touching the floor and he can't move his hands away from his face and his hands are wet and Honey has her arms around him and her face pressed down towards his and she's saying, Josh, oh, Josh, oh, love, oh, love.

She gets him on to the couch and she sits with his head on her lap and she strokes his hair until he sleeps. She moves him gently then, careful not to wake him, so that she can rise and go downstairs to the payphone in the lobby. She rings her father and he says he'll come straight away.

Her father drives as fast as he dares and leaves his car unlocked by the kerb, and as he walks into the tiny flat and sees the sleeping boy something rises from within him, a memory of perfect clarity and terrible force, and knocks him nearly from his feet.

The man glares at his daughter. Honey Bartlett, why did

you not tell me immediately that you had found this boy? Akeelia and Tasha worrying at the far sides of the world and this boy's family worrying in Ireland. And all these weeks you knew he was here and you tell no one? Why not, huh? And Honey says nothing because she's not exactly sure of the answer.

He waits for the boy to wake and he tells him his name and he tells him about a time when the boy was a baby in his mother's arms and he'd made a joke, a stupid joke, about the colour of the boy's skin. How the boy's father, his best friend, his brother, had been angry with him. How he'd bent and kissed the mother on her cheek and kissed the baby on his forehead, and told them he was sorry.

He tells the boy about a promise he'd made to himself in that moment, and to God or the universe or whatever all-powerful thing serves as the receiver of sacred promises, and accounts for the keeping or the breaking of them.

He tells the boy that he's going to take him home.

WISDOM

MOLL GLADNEY TAKES off her boots to walk the summer-heavy meadow barefoot. Picking her way through the islands of dung, the thistles and the clumps of docks, she hitches her skirt to her knees with her free hand so its hem clears the dewy grass. For comfort, for the warm safety of the ritual of it, she follows the path worn with the ages by her father around the perimeter of the Jackmans' homestead up to the brow of the small hill and down its westward slope, along the line of the lee of the hill and around the pond to where the boreen becomes a path of foot-worn earth. She pauses to pull her boots back on and pluck a handful of early blackberries but they're not yet ripe for eating and she spits the first one out and throws the rest into the pondweed. A black-feathered bird breaks from cover there and startles her as it caws skyward and she feels a pang of regret for disturbing it. She feels still in her ears and chest the rhythm of her mother's winding prayer, her low lilted novena, her whispered song of pleading. Merciful Jesus, Mother Mary, holy Saint Joseph, all the angels and saints. Bring my grandson back to me. From dawn to darkness, every day, the same imploration, obstinate, vain, filling the small house, thickening the air, settling on every surface, like a rime of heavy dust, blunting every clear line and edge so life within the yellowed walls is a blurred thing, fuzzed and imprecise, unlivable.

Along the main road two men walk, stop, lean together to confer, and walk on a few more yards, repeating these actions with a steady beat. She can't see with the wall between them what they're doing, so she walks to the stile by the gate at the cross and leans out to look. One of the men is carrying a steaming bucket and the other has a metal rectangle at the end of a long handle, and with these things they're painting white diagonal lines along the side of the road, on top of the ones that are already there, faded almost fully away. The man with the steaming bucket pours hot paint into the rectangle while his comrade deftly sweeps it along so that the lines are laid down in perfect palimpsest, new on old, and the way they work is almost hypnotic: Moll finds herself staring, then realizes they've stopped their work and are walking across the centre of the road towards a yellow lorry parked outside the shop on the far side and the one with the handled rectangle is smiling at her, and she recognizes him, remembers something about him, a distant indistinct impression, a smell of deodorant and sweat, a rough hand against her skin. She steps back from the stile and turns for home.

Her mother doesn't look up from her hearth seat when she enters through the open half-door. Ellen Jackman was here, she says. Not five minutes ago. She asked to know would you call over to her when you have time. She wouldn't stay and wait, even though I told her you'd be back in a few minutes. She's never settled, that one. She's forever on the move. I think she thinks she can dodge old age if she never stays still. She gave me a new novena but I had it got already, from Nonie Forde. I didn't tell her that, though. Best to just say thanks when someone thinks enough of you to go to any kind of trouble on your account. Pull out the two doors behind you, like a good girl. If you hurry you'll catch her crossing the meadow. She's slow enough on her feet, these days, for all her rushing. And Moll Gladney feels a flutter in her chest, a tiny fibrillation, and she turns with relief from her dried widowed mother, her fleshless drawn face, her stick-thin arms, working gently in and out as she counts off pleas bead by bead, her crucified saviour swinging up and down with the perpetual motion of her prayer, and Moll Gladney's mother barely registers the clicking latches of the door's two ancient halves as they're pulled shut.

Back out across the empty yard and past the chained and bolted shed, past the small mounds where three sheepdogs rest in their rewards, through the tiny tangled orchard, its overlong branches sagging groundward, notched and knuckled, tortured for want of pruning, she hopes as she walks, almost running, that she can catch Ellen Jackman before she crosses the meadow and clears the stile and makes it back to her own house. She wants badly to stand in the meadow with Ellen Jackman. To feel the cool sunlight, dappled through the leaves of the line of oaks at the north edge, falling on their faces and their arms. To hear Ellen Jackman ask her has she any news, knowing full well she hasn't. To hear Ellen Jackman ask does she want to walk down to Youghalarra with her later. To do a bit of weeding at the graves. And maybe stop at Conlon's well to drop a coin and say a prayer, what harm could it do, what harm is right, and Ellen Jackman's eyes will twinkle with an impish light. Moll Gladney wants in this moment, more than anything in the world, just in this moment, to clear the heavy twist of apple trees and to see ahead of her, away across the dewy meadow, crossing from the clean sunlight of the open field into the shadow of the line of oaks, the straight back of Ellen Jackman, the bare white skin of her muscled calves, her hair twisted tight into a bun on top of her head, picking her steps through an archipelago of thistles and dung, just as Moll had done herself earlier this sun-blessed morning, and to call out to her, so that Ellen Jackman stops, and turns, and smiles, and says, Ah, Moll, there you are, there you are, I was looking for you.

A new shoot whips along her bare arm as she rushes and she doesn't register immediately that her skin is torn. She sees Ellen Jackman in exactly the spot she'd imagined her in, crossing into shadow from the light, disappearing almost completely into the mottled greens and browns, merging with the oaks and ferny grass. She ups her speed and stumbles and nearly falls, and laughs at herself, at the thought of falling in the meadow in her haste to catch Ellen Jackman, of landing face first in a dried cowpat, and opening the crust of it, and of Ellen Jackman rushing back to help her up, and cleaning the cowshit from her face with a hanky from the pocket of her dress, spitting on the hanky and drawing it across her cheek with her other hand on the back of Moll's head, steadying them both, moving her hand down to cup the back of Moll's neck warmly with her strong palm and long fingers, calling her a foolish girl.

And she calls now, Ellen, wait, Ellen, and the tall woman ahead of her at the meadow's north edge stops and turns, and smiles, and says, Ah, Moll, there you are, there you are, I was looking for you. And this shadowed place is hidden from the world. No windows open on it and the field slopes up to shelter it. And there the women stand, in their long dresses, in their wellington boots, in their middle age, in their hard-won certainty of themselves, and the older woman takes the younger woman's wounded forearm in both of her hands, and lifts it to her lips, and kisses the place where the blood seeps gently through her skin.

Our Lady stands altared on a small table in Ellen Jackman's porch, a circle of tea-lights and bunches of daffodils set in slender vases around her, lilies laid bare-stemmed at her feet, a fragile diadem of chained daisies on her blue-veiled head. Moll reminds Ellen Jackman that May is long gone. You must be the only person in Ireland to leave a May altar up for a whole summer. I know, Ellen Jackman says. I can never bear to take it down. It's a stupid thing, really. My grandfather was so devoted to her. And he used to call me his Queen of the May. He'd see me coming and he'd say, Oh, here she's on, my rose of the vale, my Queen of the May, and Ellen sings, as she remembers her grandfather singing,

> *Bring flowers of the fairest*
> *Bring flowers of the rarest*
> *From garden and woodland and hillside and vale*
> *Our full hearts are swelling our glad voices telling*
> *The praise of the loveliest rose of the vale*
> *O Mary we crown thee with blossoms today*
> *Queen of the Angels, Queen of the May*

That used to rise my mother terribly. Don't be giving that one ideas about herself, she'd say. She's no spotless Blessed Lady. And I'd always check myself for spots of dirt, and would never find any, and I could never figure out what she meant. And Granddad would hold my hands in his and sing, to spite her,

> *Oh! Thus shall we prove thee,*
> *How truly we love thee,*
> *How dark without Ellen*
> *Life's journey would be!*

Ellen is still and her right hand is on her heart as she smiles into a moment of her past. And Mammy would be boiling up, her face would be as red as a berry and she'd be banging things about the place, pots off the worktop, her rolling pin smashing down on dough, and she'd be muttering about how it was flying in the face of almighty God to be changing the words of a hymn like that, it was tantamount to blasphemy, but she'd never let fly fully at him, she'd keep some sort of a lid on it because she was wary enough of him all the same. Lord, he was mad about me, though, Granddad was.

A door opens and shuts far down the dark hallway from the porch and the altar and the two barefoot women holding hands, and they separate instinctively, and each realizes they hadn't consciously taken the other's hand: it was just a thing that had become natural, unforced, their easy fondness, their unstilted companionship, and each feels in that moment the breath of danger – there's still a risk. They can't just do whatever they feel like doing. Bridget Wills the home help could easily have driven into the yard behind them and seen them through the glass of the porch. The truth of things wouldn't necessarily have occurred to her: something so outlandish would surely be beyond the scope of the imagination of a dutiful, narrow-focused, hard-working countrywoman like Bridget Wills, but still and all, it certainly would have seemed strange to her, Ellen Jackman and Moll Gladney holding hands in front of a May altar, and Ellen singing her foolish heart out and Moll looking adoringly at her, and there was no knowing the types of equations that might run in a person's head, and how they might resolve. It pays to be careful, they both well know, to guard a secret jealously, especially one so precious.

Lucas Jackman shuffles, slippered and bent-backed and slow, from the gloom of the lower corridor around the foot of the stairs and into the sunlit conservatory. He stops and regards the women impassively, nods, and shambles on towards the garden. Silent since his accident, docile and baby-like. Moll draws from her memory a picture of him as a tall, fair-haired man, freckled and tanned, with rangy limbs and calloused hands, driving a long, dark car, wearing a white shirt with the sleeves rolled up past his elbows, pulling up beside her as she walks the main road home from secondary school on a day she's missed the bus because Sister Loretta has kept her in for some small transgression and made her play scales on the upright piano at the back of the classroom for nearly an hour, slapping a ruler off her fingers each time she misses a note or presses a wrong key, and of his strange half-smile as he tells her to jump in, and of the way he looks behind him, as he stops the car by the halfway gate on the boreen, and over to his left and right, before saying, Come here, Moll, lean over towards me a second, and of his eyes, shining with some bluey-green light and his hand moving to her shoulder, quickly and suddenly, and of being pulled towards him and his mouth pressing on hers, his rough dry lips, and his free hand pushing between her

185

legs and cupping her, and letting go, and pushing her away, and laughing, a surprised laugh, as though he hadn't known he was going to do what he had done. Saying, Go on, I'll see you later. Tell your father drop in to me when he has time.

He's going to respite on Friday, Ellen says, for ten days. And she reaches for her lover's palm and squeezes it gently. Bridget will be on shortly and we'll go for our walk. And they sit in the bright kitchen and drink tea and they watch Lucas through the window, patrolling the edges of the lawn, his hands clasped behind his back, looking for all the world, from this distance and from this angle, like a man in the full of his health, his back bent only because he wishes to take in more closely the flowers' scents as he considers a problem, or inwardly philosophizes, or ruminates on the affairs of his day, or thinks about the girl he gives a lift to sometimes, the daughter of his friend and neighbour and employee, who he's been trying to seduce, by any means, force, fear, or favour, ever since she came to her fullness.

Once Bridget is in and briefed and Lucas is settled in his chair by the bay window of the good room, Ellen and Moll walk down the long poplar-lined avenue, through the open gate and out onto the main road, waiting for a line of cars to pass before they cross. Where do they all think they're going? Ellen wonders aloud, and Moll shakes her head because she doesn't know. Home from town, she supposes. Or out to the lake. Everyone in a rush, intent only on their destination. Walking downhill to Youghalarra is easy, and there's a gentle breeze on their faces, and pigeons coo in ditches and swallows flit and swoop and dash low to the ground in the fields to their left and right, and

Ellen says, It's a bad sign of the weather to see them catching flies so low, and Moll says, Dad used to say that too. He knew all the signs, the colours of the sunset, the way hares and foxes and stoats would act, the number of spiders' webs across the orchard in the mornings, the thickness of their strands, loads of things like that. And Ellen laughs at her memories of Paddy Gladney's predictions, the comically didactic tone of his voice, the absolute certainty that would be in it regardless of his past inaccuracies, and the way he'd emphasize his oracles with his bony finger, pointing it skyward, invoking the gods as he pedalled away down the lane on his post-office bicycle, the end of his right trouser leg tucked inside his sock for fear it'd catch in the chain. There was a time, she supposes, when the height of a man's abstract worries was the likelihood of rain, and the height of his immediate worries was whether his trouser leg might get oil-stained or, God forbid, ripped.

They pass the graveyard, not ready yet to bend their backs to the task of pulling weeds, resolving to double back as soon as they have a prayer said at the holy well. They turn off the road before it begins to slope steeply downwards to the quay, and onto a track of beaten earth, smoothed with the centuries by the pagans and penitents and mendicants of their parish. The trees on their left side have been cut since last they visited this place, and the hedgerow has been shaped and lowered to half its previous height or less. On a rise in the centre of the newly visible field they can see a ring fort, its protective earthen mound blunted and diminished with the ages but still clearly visible, and its circle of sentinel trees, and they marvel at the realization that they have the best part of a hundred years between them lived in this part of the world and never a thing known to them about this ancient dwelling place, this palace of fairies.

My father was always convinced that his own father died young because of a fairy ring, Ellen tells Moll. He uprooted a stand of oaks from the centre of it and levelled its earthen banks, using one of the first diesel-powered diggers in the country. Showing off, he was, his wealth and his disdain for superstition. He lost half his wealth shortly afterwards in a game of cards, and his life not long after that when his tractor overturned on a slope, just above the levelled fairy fort. My father never again spoke to our neighbours on the west side of our land on account of most of their land once being part of his inheritance, and every single bite they put in their mouths and every stitch of their clothes being owed to the foul turn of a card. He couldn't bear gambling his whole life. He went into town and kicked up a stink when the council gave permission for a betting shop to be opened on Barrack Street. He said the devil himself was behind the enterprise and that all involved would be cursed. The council listened away but they only laughed at him behind their hands. But still and all there were plenty heeded him and stayed away for years. He had a loud voice, my father had, for all his gentleness.

Moll listens to Ellen talk, nodding and humming and laughing here and there. She feels light when they walk together, suffused with pleasure and warmth, tingling, talking about things that have no weight or consequence any more, the ways of people long dead, some scandal that happened to people only vaguely known to them, something that happened in town, or on the news, far away from their small sphere of existence, the paths they wear daily, through their few fields and

188

their hillside and down a few stretches of country road, along the bank of a tributary river to the shore of the lake, their tiny green universe, its bounds drawn along the borders of a townland, their secret love its central singularity. But sadness dwells always on the periphery of her consciousness, and always gathers itself eventually and presents itself front and centre, throwing her orbit out of shape. Joshua is always near them, tagging behind or running headlong before them, excited by the sight of the water of the lake on the low horizon, sparkling in the gaps between trees, or the prospect of climbing into the handball alley to make echoes against its high wall, or of lying on his belly by the edge of the holy well, peering into its still black depths, asking, Does it really go down to the middle of the earth? Oh, yes, right down to the middle and straight through to the other side, so that it comes out again in Australia, and there could easily be a little boy like you looking into this same water right now. And Alexander is always loping long-legged beside them, quiet, smiling Alex, so content with so little, seeing no badness in anyone, seeing no danger. And Lucas is always hulking about them, eyeing them silently, brooding, filling up with darkness and resentment.

And she knows there's a danger, after his furious emigration, after all this time of silence, that she'll never see Joshua's lovely face again, or hear his sweet voice. She knows the gaps that can open between people, and the depths they can run to, and she hears still his parting shots, the words he spat at her, blaming her for his father's death, saying, Dad knew, you know, he fucking knew you didn't love him, he wouldn't have spent every minute of every day working if you'd loved him like he loved you, and she hears her own voice, weak and shocked, saying, That's not true, love, that's not true, and she wonders why she didn't follow him down the boreen, catch him at the middle gate, and wrap herself around him so he couldn't leave.

And she knows for certain she'll see no more of Alexander in this world because he's lying beside her father in a tree-shaded plot in a corner of Youghalarra graveyard, among all the dead Gladneys, and she's glad they're together there, the two great friends, the match-goers, the gardening companions, safe now from all harm.

Come on, Ellen says now, we'll walk in around it for a look. And Moll is nervous suddenly. The owner of this field isn't known to them: it's part of the old estate, and no one was ever certain of its succession, or whether the Land Commission had taken it, or whether it was being farmed at all, and it most likely was in the hands of Protestants, or the rich foreigners who'd moved in during the eighties and somehow annexed the fore-shore and the fields and forests that sloped to the lake, built walls through ancient rights of way, fenced off land that was always commonage. There could be a bull or anything, one of those monstrous English breeds. Oh, for God's sake, Ellen says, as she swings her leg over a newly erected gate in a cleared gap halfway down the path to the holy well. Come on, will you, and stop being so afraid all the time. We'll walk in and see can we find any fairies. And Moll follows, slower than her lover, less inclined to cross through this portal, this apparitional entrance to an alien place. Ellen is halfway across to the ring fort now, and she's laughing back at Moll, saying again, Come on, will you, you're some slowcoach, and her worried ghosts evanesce again, settle back to a liminal, recessed place, and Ellen shimmers before her, and disappears for a few seconds, and a scream forms itself in Moll's chest and threatens to erupt from her before Ellen appears again, and Moll realizes it was a trick of the light, a cloud rolling away from the face of the sun.

At the foot of the fort's timeworn bank Moll Gladney stands and looks at Ellen Jackman above her at the top of the mound, and she imagines her as a warrior queen, standing on the rampart of her stockade, guarding her cattle and her children and her slaves; she imagines the thin stick Ellen has pulled from a thicket and holds loose in her left hand as a sword, and she watches Ellen's loosened hair lift and fall with the gentle wind as she surveys the ditch between the bank of the fort and its ancient fosse, and she hears nothing now but the chorus of birdsong and the rustling breeze, and through those sounds Ellen's voice, saying, Look, Moll, that's where they'd have lived, right in the middle where those trees are. Come on, we'll go in.

And Moll admonishes herself for allowing herself such foolish notions, for her stupid romantic daydream, for allowing an infelicitous wave of desire to wash through her, and she climbs to the rampart and Ellen holds out her hand to help her up, though Moll would have been fully able to hoist herself unaided to the top, and Ellen grips her hand tightly as they descend into the motte of the fort and up the fosse to the clover-soft inner circle, and they stand in the shade of the three oaks that have taken root there in the heart of this Bronze Age home, and the air is still and the earth is damp and cool beneath their feet, and Ellen lets go of Moll's hand and points her stick in an arc around and says, Imagine all the lives that were lived in here, all the children born and cows milked and chickens fed and deaths met, and not a trace now of those people, no mark for their graves, no knowing where their bones are laid. Are they underneath us, I wonder? And Moll looks down at the tangle of green at her feet and when she looks up Ellen is smiling at her, and her stick has been cast away, and she takes Moll's hand again and they walk to the sunless centre of the fort, to the midpoint of the triangle of oaks where the ground is heavy and rich and smoothed by summering cattle, and every sound is drowned now by their quickened pulses, even the birdsong and the wind, and they draw each other close until their bodies touch, and their lips meet, and Moll feels the same thrill she felt the first time they kissed, on a faraway September evening as they gathered windfalls, kneeling in the orchard, seized suddenly by a tumult of love.

THE MEN WERE spreading lime and seed on the far side of the hill that day and Ellen's daughters were scattered across the country: one at Guides; one at choir practice; one at camogie. Kit was in the kitchen at her ledgers and her cashbooks, cursing quietly as she tried to make her handful of clients balance out. Moll and Ellen were filling baskets with windfalls at the meadow end of the orchard, away from the cottage, exclaiming here and there as they put their hands unwittingly on maggoty apples, or uncovered crawling wasps, flightless and drunk on ferment. Moll was wearing the new jeans her mother had bought her in town and she was worried that she'd muddy the knees of them and so she was kneeling on a rug, rising to move it forward as she moved steadily along the walkway through the trees, where most of the apples landed when they fell. Ellen Jackman, moving against her, intent also on saving the wind's harvest, lost her balance as she bent earthward and fell forward, and reached out a hand to steady herself, and her hand landed on Moll, on the soft flesh of her side, and Moll grabbed her hand and they were kneeling facing one another, and they were kissing, and the sweetness of their kiss vied with the shock of the fact of it in Moll Gladney's head, and she was entirely lost to it for a full minute or more before fear came between them, and they broke from each other and Moll was on her feet, and she lifted her full basket and carried it to her mother's kitchen, and Ellen didn't call her back, just rose and carried her own basket across the meadow home.

Moll Gladney wrote a letter to Ellen Jackman the next day and she put a stamp on it and posted it in the post office and she allowed a fortnight for an answer to come, and when none did she rose early one morning and she left her parents' house and took the factory bus to town and the train to Dublin and sailed to Wales and bussed to London and it was five years before she laid eyes on Ellen Jackman again.

LATER BY THE holy well they pray, Moll kneeling at the spring's stone lip, beseeching for her absent son and the souls of her father and her husband and for her mother's wounded heart, and Ellen standing beside her seeking intercession for her own children, and for her dark wounded husband, and each for the other's intentions, and each for the forgiveness of their own sins, and Ellen drops a pound coin into the black water and says, That'll do the two of us. Lord knows we've a couple of ransoms thrown in there with the years. And what a waste, when you think about it. Firing money into a puddle in the ground and we damned anyway no matter what we do. Does anyone ever come and take it out? And Moll doesn't answer, because she doesn't know and doesn't care: she's shaking still a little from her lover's touch; the ground around the well seems bumpier than usual, she has to be careful where she puts her feet or she might fall.

The sacrifice is the main thing, Ellen supposes, and Moll nods and Ellen's hand now is on the back of her head, and she's saying how well we had to end up here, still here, after all our big talk. For all the places we went in our heads we got nowhere in truth. But anyway. We are where we are, as the smart ones say. And Moll rises slowly to her feet and resists the impulse to take Ellen's hand because they're in the open now; for all the seclusion of the well, they're on common land, and a neighbour could at any moment breach the bounds of this blessed place, and the Blessed Lady cast of stone that guards the well has a more forbidding expression than the white and sky-blue alabaster Mother of Ellen Jackman's shrine. She doesn't look as though she'd be impressed. Moll considers for a moment weaving a chain of daisies as a crown for the cold stone Virgin's head, then decides against it: Ellen has already started back towards the path to the quay road and, anyway, May is gone.

Do you really think we are? Moll asks, and her sudden question jolts Ellen from a pleasant reverie. Are what? Ellen asks. Damned, says Moll. But Ellen is silent. She needs time to form an answer. She's been thinking about the ten days of freedom they're going to have when Lucas goes to respite care, twenty-five miles away in Patrickswell. She hopes none of her children will ring to say they are coming to stay, or even to visit for a day; she knows it's unlikely but, still, there's always a chance that her anticipated idyll will be shattered, that her grandchildren, as beautiful as they are, will impose their noisy, wailing, hungry selves on her time of grace. She can't bear the thought of her daughters or her son arriving in their gigantic cars with travel-cots and pushchairs and changing mats and bicycles and scooters and powders and potions and all sorts of alien accoutrements, their awkwardly polite and strangely accented spouses in tow, tramping through the middle of her sacred week and a half, her very occasional chance to open her door fully to the truth of herself. Her home is decorated softly now, in a way that speaks of Moll, in the colours and styles that she knew would please her love, and no one else alive can ever know that. Her home is Moll's home too, as scarce as their days or nights together are; her life is Moll's life and that's all there is to it.

One of Moll's paintings hangs on the wall of her good room, of a willow tree, its branches cascading towards a pool of still water, its leaves backlit bright yellow and green by the sun. Two of Moll's seascapes hang in her bedroom, one above her bed of a calm sea beneath a blue sky flecked with puffs of white cloud and one across from the foot of her bed of an angry sea beneath a heavy grey sky with a row of black cliffs stretching away to the horizon on the left side, and she lies some nights listening to Lucas's snores from his room next door, just looking at the dark sea in that picture, the water churning blue-black tipped in white, marvelling at Moll's fine hand, picturing her as she must have looked while she painted it, in her makeshift studio in the cottage, in the extension Paddy built with Alexander's help, her face lit by the sun through the skylight.

Her children are well reared and educated, capable and confident and adjusted, and her three daughters are, truth be told, bossy little bitches, full of their opinions and beliefs and eye-rolling incredulity at their mother's innocence, at her faithful observance, her adherence to certain rituals and sacraments, her anachronistic ways. Her son is never out of the sky, it seems, flying here and there, over and back across the globe, doing all sorts of deals for the bank he works for, the one named for a city, a name that always eludes her. Ellen knows her son will never farm the land. He'd leased it out as soon as he'd been given power of attorney, and she was glad. She knows full well the breakdown of Lucas's will – she'd been present for the making of it: his estate in its entirety will pass to his only son, with a leasehold for life on the house to be granted to Ellen if he predeceases her. Lucas provided for a gift to each of the girls on their reaching of their majority and considered his duty by them done. The land is to stay in Jackman hands, to be passed along the male line, and no argument will be brooked, or any offered. Dunbar the solicitor had wheezed something at them about Ellen having a legal-right share under the Succession Act of 1955 to one-third of the estate were she to assert that right but Lucas had laughed at this, and told Dunbar to stop talking rubbish, and Dunbar had looked at her and smiled, sadly, she thought. And Lucas then had raised his voice and told the solicitor to do as he was instructed or forget about his business. There's plenty more where you came from, he said, only mad looking for clients. There's a street of you people here, looking out of your windows through your books. And Dunbar had sighed and raised his palms and said he'd draw it up post haste.

But Ellen had never foreseen her only son's generosity. She feels still the thrill of pride she first felt when he drove into the yard with a yellow padded envelope containing a thin sheaf of fresh paper: a newly drawn-up deed for the Gladneys' cottage, and a map with the cottage and the orchard and gardens outlined in red, a freehold in the name of Kathleen Gladney, out-right ownership with no limit of time, with only an easement retained to allow unimpeded use of the boreen, with a stipula-tion that same would be paved and maintained at his continuing expense. To come into effect with the weight of law on his father's death. She remembers how his cheeks flushed when she told him how proud she was of him, that she loved him, that he was after doing something beautiful and incredible. How he'd mumbled something about it being the least he could do: the Gladneys had always been good friends to them, they'd given so much of themselves to the Jackmans, they'd lost so much. She remembers still the tears on Kit's face, her embarrassed joy, and her whispered words: He'll have something to come back to now. She remembers how Kit embraced him, and the happy look in Andrew's eyes when she laid her hand on his cheek and told him he was a wonderful boy. How he'd deflected this praise, saying, It was always yours, Kit, yours and Paddy's. This only makes it official.

She loves all of her children dearly, and she misses them, and she worries about them terribly, but still she prays they'll stay away, just for this next little while. And at least she has an answer for Moll. Damned? Ellen laughs and says, I don't know. We'll have a few questions to answer for sure. They'll want to know what we thought we were doing, I'd say, what got into us. And my answer will be the same as yours will be – we had no choice in the matter. Don't worry, my love, I'll be gone a good bit ahead of you and I'll have your story told for you along with my own and all your apologies well made. I'll be waiting for you with a clean sheet to begin eternity. And if there's nothing more beyond this it won't bother us one bit because we won't know which or whether. And anyway, if we're to believe what we're told, isn't everything divine? Weren't the lines of all maps drawn long before we lived? We are but actors on a stage, my sweetheart. And Moll says, Oh, I don't know. Let's not talk about dying. I couldn't bear the thought of it if you were gone, I don't know what I'd do. And Ellen laughs again and says, What are we like at all? and they turn from the quay road into the graveyard entrance, and separate there to tend their respective dead.

As she takes her gardening gloves from their cubby-hole behind a loose block at the foot of the graveyard's outside wall, Ellen thinks about another sunny evening three years ago, when the universe turned in on itself and compressed itself back to a singularity of darkness and opened itself again and was full of light. She sees it and hears it and feels it in her memory in perfect crawling detail. The heady harvest smell of early autumn in the evening air as she walked the long path from the far side of the hill up the edge of the pond bound for the Gladneys' cottage with a half-dozen jars of preserves wrapped in a top-knotted muslin cloth. The innocence of her thoughts, her ignorance, almost happy, mapping in her head her coming week. The chill that struck the core of her and worked outwards to her skin when she heard the muffled crying and a voice, rough and familiar, threatening.

The sudden stillness of the evening, the feeling of time itself being broken. The heaviness of her steps as she climbed the last few yards to the gate and leant on its top rail and looked right, where the field stretched green along the curve of the hill and banked down to the valley, then forced herself to look left to where an ancient oak stood, one she'd heard was once a hanging tree. She saw Moll with her back against the tree, Lucas Jackman facing her. The green branches arcing down nearly obscuring them. The sound of Lucas Jackman carried true to her ears on the midsummer breeze, on air that rolled fresh from the ocean, tracked upriver to the lake and onto this mountainside. She heard his words, coming in short bursts, matching the rhythm of his inward and outward movement, Now, you fucking bitch, you'll learn your lesson, about the way these things are meant to be, about the way things work between women and men, you'll learn the lesson now your husband couldn't teach you, you'll learn now, girl, and you have this lesson coming to you a long time. Lucas Jackman's moon-white arse, Moll's hands pummelling his body and slapping open-palmed into the side of his face, Lucas drawing back from her, closing his right hand on her throat and flinging her bodily to the ground beneath the tree, onto the hard grassless earth worn level and smooth by summering cattle, his grisly pirouette as he turned and flung himself down on top of her, Moll's arms out now at her sides, surrendering, it seemed. She felt a cry strangled in her own throat, and a heaviness in her legs as they carried her over the gate and into the field, and the thick grass of the Long Acre beneath her rushing feet, and the heft of the jars of preserves in their bag of cloth, and the fastness of her grip on the wound neck of it, and the ease of the upward swing of her arm as she ran, and the sureness of her timing of her swing. She saw the flare of shock and fright in Lucas's eyes as he looked up just in time to see the coming of his doom. The mighty crack of glass on bone. His body slumped and prone. The seeping jam like blood, the darkening earth. Moll Gladney weeping on the ground. Ellen Jackman kneeling beside her, holding her, saying, It's all right, my love, it's all right.

REVELATION

In her cottage Kit Gladney is praying still. She can get only the barest feel of her grandson, the faintest sense of him, and no certainty of his wellbeing or his whereabouts. He's lost for the time being beyond any kind of finding. What kind of a curse was laid on her to say that this could happen twice in one life? She aches for her lost men, for Joshua and for Alexander and for Paddy, and the pain's long duration has done nothing to knock the keen edge from it: it's there always, on every surface, in every cranny of her kitchen and her house and the soil and stones and green grass. She aches most keenly now for Joshua, her black-haired boy, her second child. She curses herself for all the times she told him to cut his hair, put on proper clothes, stop going around like a blasted beggar man with his arse hanging out of his trousers. The times she snapped at him to put away whatever book he was reading and take out his schoolbooks instead, and told him it was more in his line to fill out a few application forms for jobs or courses besides writing things down in a notebook no one was ever allowed to read. And every time she swiped at him he'd only smile, and say, Yes, Gran, and he'd stretch his long legs across the kitchen and bend himself over pages and Paddy would come in and they'd have a big long conversation about the hurling and the football and what was in the news, and Joshua was the image of his father, and Paddy and Joshua had the same easy way between them that Paddy and Alexander used to have, before his lonesome death on the side of the road.

Kit had a touch of a thing. That was what she called it, a thing. It had a proper name, she'd been told it once, but it was one of those rubbery words that wouldn't lie straight in her memory. It didn't allow her to see the future or talk to the dead, but it was the reason for the awful sense she had that Joshua had lost himself, that he hadn't done anything foolish to himself the way so many boys his age had done, and do every day, and will do in all the days to come, but still that he was in a place of darkness. And the thing had allowed her to know that Alexander was a good man from the earliest time of her knowing him, that his love for Moll was true, that he wasn't a liar or a thief. She still regretted that Moll hadn't made more of herself, gone into the city to the school of commerce, learnt to type and to bookkeep like Kit, but life was like that: it meandered on and away along its course and there wasn't much anyone could do in the path of Fate but stand aside and hope and pray for the best.

Paddy had loved his son-in-law, too. Kit had watched it happen, slowly, over a year or so. The Englishman would arrive home in the evening from the factory all hellos and proclamations about the weather and how it weren't half bloody cold, and, Hello, Mum, and he'd bend himself nearly double to plant a kiss on the top of her head, and he'd draw in air through his great nose and declare that the smell in this house was like nothing he'd ever smelt before and what the heck was it? Apple tart? Currant cake? Ah, Kit, my love, I'd climb yon mountain, I'd swim yon lake, for just one slice of that currant cake! And he'd roll the *rs* in *currant* and he'd wait by the oven until she opened it and lifted out whatever was in it, and she'd smack the back of his hand when he reached for it, and he'd sit at the table in the kitchen and wait while the tart or the cake or the tray of scones cooled by the window and Paddy would sit across from him, and they'd talk away nineteen to the dozen. And Kit would often look out of the half-door and see him and Alexander, walking off together through the meadow, with bales of fencing wire and mallets or axes and chainsaws, off about the work of securing the perimeters of the Jackmans' land, of keeping their livestock hemmed and safe.

Alexander was the blue-black of the night sky. At first she couldn't stop looking at him. She'd never seen a black person up close, bar the few they'd encountered the day they'd gone searching for Moll in Dublin. The flat nose of him and the pinkness of his palms. The big lips. Lord, he was a sight. How Moll's whiteness had won through for Joshua against all that blackness was anyone's guess. Still, though, the boy was curly-haired and brown-eyed. Alexander wasn't quite a Protestant, he said, but he definitely wasn't a Catholic either. His parents knew reams of the Bible off by heart, he said, and they could quote it for any occasion, and he went to church and to Sunday school all through his childhood, but he'd go along with any old thing, he said, he'd learn those Catholic prayers and he'd say them with gusto, he'd lift up his heart and his soul to the Lord in praise and thanks for all he'd been given. His beautiful wife and his beautiful son. That kind of fortune would turn any face to Heaven in thanks, he said. And every Sunday morning he walked with Paddy and Kit up the long hill to Mass, and he even joined in the responses and bits and pieces of the Act of Contrition and the Our Father and the Hail Mary, and she loved the way he called her Mum, the very same as the English lads on the television. It gave her a strange thrill to be called that by a great long Englishman, as black as the ace of spades, as handsome as all get out, with a voice as soft as summer rain. What was loveliest about Alexander, though, was the way he loved Moll. The reverent way he loved her. Never loud in his love, or showy, but quiet, nervous almost, like he was afraid he was in a dream and if he wasn't careful he could accidentally wake himself.

Still, Kit had to allow that Paddy was right when he declared that Alexander was full of big talk. But what on earth was so wrong with that? It wasn't big talk about fighting or bombing or the North of Ireland or the Vietnamese Communists or anything like that: it was big talk about a site he was going to buy near the lake and the palace of a house he was going to build and how they'd all live there together, and they'd have acres of space, and he was going to have sunrooms and orange rooms and snooker rooms and all sorts of rooms, and Paddy always got vexed and asked him how a lad that put handles on saucepans for a living was going to do all this, and Alexander always tapped a long finger against his flat nose and said, Ha-ha, you wait and see, I've got some things brewing. You have in your eye, Paddy would say, laughing. You have your lot, boy. But it turned out he did have things brewing, good and careful plans made, and he started into the landscape gardening, and he was beginning to make a great go of it.

Kit untwines her fingers and makes fists of her hands now and twines her fingers again, and continues with her metronomic rosary, and she tries to prevent her thoughts from

208

overlaying themselves on her prayers but she can't. It's just one of those evenings where unbidden memories tumble to the front of her mind and impose themselves on her consciousness. Those two lovely men gone. She'd turned away from Our Lady for a good long while after Alexander went. It seemed such a mockery, for such awful things to be allowed to happen.

The man who'd hit him on the road showed up in the yard one misty morning not long after the funeral, hardly able to speak. Kit met him halfway across from the gate and he said who he was and she was inclined to run him but he stood his ground and said, I just want to say one thing to the man's wife and his little boy. Please will you let me? But they weren't there, and Kit pulled her coat around her as a kind of a defence against the man's contrition, a deflecting shroud against the pain of his guilt, and she told him he could say whatever he'd come to say and that she'd pass it on to Moll and Joshua. And the man was looking at the ground at her feet and she knew by the way he was moving them that he had no idea what to do with his hands. Eventually he met her eyes and she could see that he wasn't long out of his boyhood and his hand shook as he held it out to her, and when she took it she could feel the heat of his fear and shame. He held her hand while he spoke and she made no effort to take it back. I wasn't going that fast, he said. He was looking into her face now and there were tears in his blue eyes. He came out onto the road from the back of his trailer and I wasn't going fast, I swear on my mother and my father's life, but I shouldn't have hit him. I should have stood on the brakes and swerved across the road. But it was like I froze up or something and it didn't register in time that I was going to hit him, because he was there so sudden, and I remember thinking, That's your man, the . . . And the sound of it, the sound he made, the crack against the windscreen. And when I stopped and got out, the way he was lying. Oh, Jesus, the angle he was at in the middle of the road. And the boy stopped there, and he gathered himself.

The day after it happened I went down the riverbank with a clothesline rope to kill myself but my oul fella followed me and got me in time. I asked him then to take me into the barracks and I told Jim Gildea I wanted to be arrested and Jim said, For what in the name of Jesus, and I said, Manslaughter or something, and Jim brought me and Dad into a room inside in the barracks and he said I was to cop on to myself, that sometimes things happened that could have been prevented but there was no earthly way to change the past, there was no point in holding on to things, that the world had a funny old way of working. Then my father blurted out that I was after trying to do away with myself and it was as if Jim knew already and he said, Ah, Jesus, son. He said the one thing he knew for certain was that adding sadness to sadness could only cause more sadness. But I think I'll never stop being sad, if that's any good to you. I'll never get rid of this feeling no matter what I do. Will you tell your daughter and your grandson I'm sorry? Will you tell them my heart is broken for them and I'll never forgive myself? And my heart is broken for you too, Mrs Gladney, and I'll never be right again. If it's any good to you, I'll never again have a happy day.

And Kit put her arms around him then and, the very same as Alexander Elmwood, he had to bend nearly double into her embrace and he sobbed like a child. She could feel the weight of his grief and regret, and she knew it might even make things worse for this uncertain country boy that she was being kind, that she didn't hate him, that she could show him only love.

Paddy at least had died well. Six years after Alex. Down at the end of the garden, with the sun warm on his face, a kind breeze blowing. Among the buds and new leaves, on a bed of his fresh-cut grass, he laid himself down. As though he'd felt it coming and knew, and thought, There's nothing for it now but to lie down here. And Kit, when she finds me, will be glad I died well. And she was, and she thanked God, and she made her peace with the Blessed Lady for allowing Paddy to die among his flowers, in her lovely month of May.

ELLEN REMEMBERS NOW, as she pulls weeds and tidies the narrow lines of gravel around her family's plot in the centre of the middle section of Youghalarra graveyard, how they had gotten up from the ground and stood above her husband, then, at either side of him, and looked down, and he wasn't moving, and neither of them could think what next to do. There was an opening a palm's-length along his forehead and it was seeping blood so dark it was almost black. Ellen was certain he was dead. She looked across at Moll and held out a hand across her husband's body and Moll took her hand and it occurred to Ellen that this was only the second time in over twenty years that they had touched. Was that possible, she wondered, and the question wouldn't leave her, and she marvelled at the strangeness of her mind, how it could fix itself at this moment of danger, at this cataclysm, on the question of whether she had touched any part of the body of Moll Gladney between the time that they had kissed each other's lips in the orchard by the cottage on a September evening long ago and the moment she had taken her in her arms this warm evening. They must have shaken hands when she came back after being missing for those years. But no: Moll had quarrelled with her on that first Sunday when she'd gone to the cottage after Mass. But that had been her fault: she had barged in and given her a shock and she hadn't been kind and her opening gambit had been, Who in the name of God do you think you are? And that made no sense then and makes no sense still. But in all the years after, between that moment and this, how could they never have shaken hands or embraced or kissed? At Alexander's death or Paddy's? But for all that couldn't be answered it was a fact now that all the moments of their lives had stacked themselves together and had built themselves to this point: her husband Lucas was lying dead between them after attempting to take Moll Gladney by force beneath the old oak in the Long Acre and the choices laid before them now were suddenly clear in Ellen's head, and they were stark.

Has this happened before? Ellen asked Moll, and Moll shook her head and whispered, No. Not like this. This is as far as he's ever gone, and it's been years since he even looked at me. And Ellen wasn't sure of the truth of this but she accepted it in silence and she bent to the task of gathering her jars of preserves back into her checked cloth bag and she picked the glass of the two broken jars from the ground and she scooped the spilt jam from the earth and she dug down a little with her fingernails, though the ground was hard from the dry weather, so that no sign of any glass or jam remained, and she tied the top of her bundle tight and stopped moving for a moment to consider. The hands were all gone home. Her house was empty. Only Kit was in the cottage, and maybe Josh. Moll didn't know where Josh was. He was wild, these days, gone for days at a time to God knew where, and always so silent and surly when home, sleeping until noon and getting up and taking off again, not bothering even with his music or with hurling training or with any of his old pals, as far as she knew.

Come on, Ellen said. And she put her hand to Lucas's neck and felt no pulse, and she lowered her cheek to his lips and felt no breath on her skin, and she held his wrist in her hand and waited to feel a movement beneath the ball of her thumb and there was none and so she was satisfied that he was gone, this dark, silent man she had married, this creature who had been her gaoler and her burden and the source of all her loathing and her fear since first he'd come visiting to her parents' house.

And she took Moll's hand again and she lifted her bundle of preserves and the two women walked hand-in-hand back to the gate, and onto the path, and off it again and into the meadow, and across it to the house where Ellen lived, and Ellen told Moll what they were going to do. They took a chainsaw from the workshop. They took a ladder and a length of rope and a pair of working gloves. They hefted these things back across the meadow and Ellen opened the stepladder beneath one of the low branches of the oak tree and she primed the chainsaw and she tugged at its starter and after three times it roared into life and she held the throttle open and she held the saw outwards from herself and she climbed the steps slowly to the top and she felt her arms weaken but she lifted the saw towards the thick place where the branch met the trunk and she made a cut there, a small one just, and she cried out in pain at the chips of sawdust that stung her face and she closed the throttle and looked down at Moll, who was standing watching her, and she said to Moll to stand back, stand right back away from him, and she turned and she pitched the chainsaw into the air in the direction of Lucas's body and it landed on the ground beside him blade first and it lay dented there.

She climbed slowly down the stepladder with Moll behind

her on the ground to steady her descent and she laid the step-ladder on its side on the ground and the two women stood back for a clearer view, and Ellen decided that her arrangement of body, saw and ladder was convincing: anyone surveying the scene would have only one conclusion available to them. For whatever reason, Lucas Jackman had decided to cut the low branches from the old oak at the centre of the south perimeter of the hilltop field on his land known as the Long Acre, and in doing so had fallen from his ladder and had sustained a head injury in the fall and had died.

Now, as she kneels with her hand pressed to a cold head-stone and grasps a clump of thistle and pulls slowly and firmly so that it leaves the earth, root and all, Ellen remembers the lightness she had felt in that moment, the wonderful unbur-dening. She was crying and so was Moll beside her but there was no grief, just a lifting of a dark mass from above her and around her, a clearing of the sky, a bursting through of light and hope. Moll's hand was in hers and it fitted well and was warm and they walked in silence back to the path and Ellen told Moll to go home to the cottage, to act as though nothing had happened. And she dialled 999 from the phone on the hall table and she shouted into the receiver that there'd been an accident, her husband had fallen, that she thought he was dead. And she ran at full stretch back across the meadow so she'd be breathless and sweating if anyone was there before her, and she composed as she ran the lines that she would say, the timeline of her discovery of Lucas lying beneath the tree, of checking his vital signs, of ascertaining that he had no pulse, of shouting for help to no avail, because who was nearby to hear her shouts? How her own house was empty because her children were all away and the farmhands had finished for the day and not even the Gladneys were close enough and anyway they had no phone. Of deciding she had to leave him and run for the phone to call an ambulance and then run back to continue her chest compressions just in case, and she knew her procedure and her lingo well because she had trained a few years as a nurse before her father had told her she was to come home out of it and she was to do what was expected of her, and Lucas Jackman was a fine man from the best of stock, from the richest of land, and once she was married to him there'd be no question of her working outside the home, as a nurse or anything else.

And she remembers how the sky closed over again, how the dark mass gathered again and pressed down over her when the shocker was taped to Lucas's bared chest and switched on; how the mass had constricted itself around her when the ambulance man turned to his comrade and said, There's a pulse. And they put a mask on Lucas's face and a blanket over him and they continued to perform compressions in turns while Jim Gildea and another guard, a young fellow from Westmeath or Kildare or somewhere, stood either side of her and asked her over and over again was she okay, did she want to sit down, did she want to go in the helicopter when it came, there'd more than likely be room for her, and the boreen and the path and the edges of the field filled with neighbours, and she heard children cheering as the helicopter landed on the swaying summer grass.

And she feels the evening breeze light and chill on her neck now, bare because her long hair is all drawn to one side as she kneels on the hard sunned earth, and she hears a whisper on the breeze, as she always does, reminding her of all her lies, of all her sins. All the days and weeks waiting for Lucas to waken fully, with doctors telling her his signs were good, his heart was strong, his oxygen was high; he was rallying stronger every day, but still she shouldn't expect too much. The blood that had pooled at the site of his injury was drained away, a cut had been made at the side of his skull to ease the pressure of the swelling there, but his was a life-changing injury. When he came back from it he'd come back changed. All the times she'd sat alone at his bedside, thinking, It'd only take a minute. A hand tight across his mouth, her forefinger and her thumb pinching his nostrils hard closed. She remembers the plan she made with Moll one Sunday while they listened to Mass being piped through speakers into the hospital's wards. To take her savings from the building society and run. To disappear into the world, somewhere sun-drenched and blue-skied. The same plan, give or take, that Moll had made and written in a letter to her once. But how could she have left her children? She had memorized the letter and then burnt it over the sink, and Moll had gone without her, and left no word behind, before she'd ever replied.

She remembers the day Lucas woke, and the deadness in his eyes, and the gathering relief as assessment after assessment came back the same. A semi-vegetative state. A walking, waking death.

Eternity be damned. She'd done her time in Hell, and so had Moll.

MOLL THINKS ALWAYS of Alexander sleeping as she tidies his grave. She thinks of him whole and intact, having a pleasant dream, a slight smile on his lips. How he looked as he lay beside her, holding her hand sometimes, always sleeping so silently and still. He was easy to share a bed with for such a big man. He never tossed or turned, just lay on his back and slept, and his face was so beautiful in the peace of sleep that she sometimes felt a yearning stir inside her, some kind of a rare drawing towards him, and she woke him on those occasions with a kiss, and moved her hand along the length of him to let him know he could turn to her. And she loved the slow and gentle way he moved, and she loved the happy light in his eyes, and she hated herself for controlling him this way, for allowing him so little of herself, but she knew that he'd be happy with less, with next to nothing at all, if he could only be near her. She always thinks of how she used him. How he let himself be used. How his love for her was so complete and hers for him so brittle and so weak. What faulty magic cast these things she didn't know, what terrible arrangement of their stars.

She couldn't see a reason for his love, for the way he fell for her. She thought at first he was just the same as other men she'd walked with, that he'd do his best to talk her sweetly round but failing that would press his case roughly, that she'd have to struggle and threaten and cry before he'd leave her be. He waited for her after every shift she worked, to see her safely home to her boarding house. He looked for favours from all his workmates so he could be free to walk with her, and, she was told, always paid them back double what they were owed in money and time. He said her name softly, and always smiled as he spoke. Moll. My Irish Molly-oh. He learnt songs from immigrant neighbours and sang them to her sweetly as they walked. He somehow found out some words of Irish and he enunciated them slowly and proudly: *dee-a-gwit, cun-ass-a-taw-too*, Alexander – *iss-annum-dum, taw-too-guh-hawl-een*. That last one means, You're lovely, he'd tell her. And he'd learnt the word for beautiful. *Daw-hool. Taw-too-daw-hool-a-store.* He told her he'd asked how to say I love you and he was told there was no way of doing so, there was no direct translation of those words into Irish. He didn't believe this. He asked her and asked her if that was true, and she tried to remember her lessons from school, the voice of the thin nun who'd taught them by rote, and she couldn't hear in her memory the nun ever teaching them such a thing; she couldn't even remember the word for *love* and she snapped at him that no one really spoke Irish any more except in schools and a few wild spots out west and that those words he was saying made no sense and how would she know anyway? But still he laughed softly and walked beside her, and left her at her doorway every night, and asked nothing else of her.

She thought she could pray her way out of her own desires, out of the curse she'd been burdened with. She thought she could ask for intercession from the saints – and was it really a lot to ask? – in helping her to overcome this need she had to touch another woman, to kiss another woman's lips, a woman she had known since childhood, who lived across a wide meadow from her house, and across a wider divide than could ever be bridged by any imposturous impulse. And in the end she'd let him make love to her, and then she'd married him, because she could do nothing else. And in the end she loved him in a way, because she could do nothing else. And still she left him, and ran for home, because she couldn't let her soul be twisted any further out of shape.

Moll was afraid of the child, of his steady, knowing gaze, of the ancient wisdom he seemed silently to hold. She didn't feel deserving of a thing so beautiful, so perfect. She was afraid for him. A strange force of terror and love seemed to take over her entire being when she looked at his face and saw herself reflected in his eyes, a conviction that she was poised on the edge of some abyss, the push of a hand from a cataclysm, from destruction. This terror seemed to shake the inside of her; it seemed sometimes to pitch and roll and break over her in wave after crashing wave, and at other times to calm and flatten out and stretch away to infinity.

She was disturbed by his whiteness, by the upset this had caused. She'd expected he'd be black or so brown at least as to pass for black; she saw no possibility that her whiteness would be passed in its fullness to the child. Friends and neighbours of the Elmwoods tutted and shook their heads and told strange and terrifying stories of changelings and demons that travelled on ships and cursed children. Delilah shouted at them to check their tongues, to keep their foolish mouths shut. And still she was able to leave him, to rise one early morning and make Alexander's breakfast and see him off to work and walk down the stairs to Barney and Delilah and ask them to take the baby for an hour or two at most while she went out to run a few small errands. And they were so happy to oblige her and they showered her with blessings as she left and she felt not even a twinge of regret or guilt as she doubled back to fetch her suitcase from the stairwell and leave lying there a hurried note of apology, and take a city bus to Victoria coach station and the international service home.

And of course he found her, and what could she do about that? And his touch was always gentle, and his lovemaking was always a form of worship, and still she couldn't reason out his mind, still she couldn't fathom the depth of his love for her. And she regrets now the shallowness of her pretences with him. That she didn't act her role with more aplomb. That she always lay so silent and so still, and made him feel almost as though he'd taken her against her will, until in the end he stopped trying, and contented himself with lying beside her, kissing her shoulder before he slipped into dreams. She helped him with her hand sometimes and he always thanked her afterwards, and wiped away his issue quickly and embarrassedly. She hoped sometimes he'd take up with somebody else. She saw the way some women looked at him. She'd heard the whispers and the talk, the bawdy conjecture. Moll Gladney's black bull and what he might do to you.

Moll pushes out all thoughts of Josh, and silences the voices in her head, accusing her. Why did you not talk to the boy? Why did you not make sure he was okay? Why didn't you ask him and ask him and ask him to tell you how he was feeling, to tell you how terribly he missed his daddy, to tell you how much the world hurt him? How had she let the world hurt him so much? She tries to think about the coming week and the walks she'll take across the meadow to the house of her lover and the bed where she will lie with her, and they'll close and padlock the driveway gate and they'll listen to the distant silage-making and know that it's no concern of theirs, that there'll be no cooking or baking or tea-making to be done for hungry and thirsty and sunburnt men. She tries to lie. To tell herself that Josh is in a strop. That all she must do is wait and someday he'll return, and he'll smile at her, and the sadness will be gone from his eyes. She reads and rereads the one letter he sent, saying he was sharing a house with some lads from Clare, and they weren't the worst, and that he was playing music in pubs at night, and that he was working in a hotel by day, and that she wasn't to worry one bit about him. She tries and tries to tell herself that he's just young, and thoughtless, and that the chances are he never has the money for the phone, or the time or inclination to sit and write a letter. That he's cross with her for all the reasons, real and intangible, that a boy without his father will have for being cross with his mother. That his granddad's death was too much extra grief for him to stay here and bear, surrounded every moment by reminders of him, and of his father, of the good men and their work, their walls and fences and their blooming flowers and thick-limbed trees.

She regrets the way she turned on Ellen Jackman, and blamed her for her contorted existence. When all along the truth was clear and plain that Moll was a coward. But what kind of strength would it have taken to tell the truth of things? The women meet again at the graveyard wall and they hide their gloves and weeding tools behind the loose stone where they've always hidden them, for as long as they've been tending together these graves. Ellen touches Moll's hand as they kneel and tells her she'll need a minute before she can get up, that she feels a little dizzy. Moll's heart quickens in her chest with fear. What if this is a sign of something else? She's always thought this way about happiness, and so far she's always been right. It doesn't last because it can't. She supposes this is why people cleave so hard to faith, to the idea of love and life ever-lasting, of eternal grace. She supposes this to be the case for everyone, this fear of things ending, this pall that's cast by life's very nature, its pitiful situation, set between two infinities. And further there's the worry of her kith and kind, of damnation, this supernatural threat she can't cast off. This blazing love she shares with Ellen Jackman might inversely be a punishment: their victory in the battle for these fleeting joys might well by pyrrhic; they might well scorch and burn for ever as payment for these sins. She checks herself closely in this moment of fear, with Ellen head-bowed beside her, regaining her steadiness before she gets to her feet, and finds that she doesn't care. She'll face God or the devil or any envoy of theirs and she'll look them in their eye and she'll endure whatever torments they see fit to make her suffer.

MOLL AND ELLEN have their ten blissful days together, and they're left in peace, and the summer cools and the days contract, and Lucas Jackman dies quietly in his sleep as the season turns, and he's buried, and his children mourn, and a smallholding in Knockagowny passes in law to Kit Gladney, and the world spins on. One sharp morning at the start of autumn, in the kitchen of the cottage on the side of a hill where she's lived all of her married life and all of her widowed life, Kit Gladney sits at her ancient table of warm and heavy oak. She has her rosary beads in her hands and she's working her way automatically along the decades and the cup of tea she poured is getting cold because she's had a visit from Paddy, and she can smell him and feel the energy of him and his quiet unstinting love filling the room from wall to wall and ceiling to floor, and it's a joy, pure and simple, it's Heaven on earth to sit here like this, surrounded, suffused. And she thanks God for allowing her this, and feels deserving of it, and is pricked then by guilt for considering herself to be deserving of anything, and she feels the cold breath of the deadly sin of pride and she chides herself for worrying about such things and she pushes all her fear away and relaxes into her vision. Because Paddy's visits come sometimes like that: like dreams, scenes of things that sometimes make no sense but are always bathed in a soft light that she knows is him, suffusing everything.

This intermittent extra sense has never cost her too much thought or ever given her too much earthly help. But it's sharpened in these years of grief, like a blade milled on a whetstone to a keen edge. She started to feel the rising strength of it in the empty quiet time after Paddy went, when all the waking and the public mourning were done and the house had emptied and the briars had started to reach from the hedgerow again and across the path up to her gate because Paddy wasn't there bodily to hold back the growth and she hadn't ever fully realized how much work it took, how much the good man laboured every day to keep their small stead tidy and pristine, and Joshua was gone each day to school and Moll was at her jobs, and she started to know for a plain and hard and joyful truth that Paddy was still with her. In prayer she'd close her eyes and drift sometimes to thought, and memory, and she'd picture every line and mark of Paddy's face for fear she'd forget him, and she'd smell him and she'd feel the draught of him passing her and she wouldn't dare open her eyes for fear the spell would break. And he would show her things sometimes, to ease her mind. He let her know that Moll is happy now at last, and that her happiness is tied fast to her friendship with Ellen Jackman, and that things happened on this hillside that never should have happened, and other things happened that atoned in some way for these things, that balanced some fragile scales, and Paddy drew only a scant outline of these things, and she knew this land held secrets that even Paddy in his grace could not show her. But wasn't that true of every place on God's earth? And she knows, from the sight of her own eyes and the

225

two ears God gave her, as convinced as they are that their secret is just between the two of them, that what passes daily between Moll and Ellen is a rare and precious thing, and as familiar to her as her own hand and yet as unknowable to her as the workings of the insides of the stars.

She heard a priest one time explain eternity that way in her childhood, a fierce and terrifying man. Time has no meaning there, he said, because how can it? How can there be a unit of infinity? And so all your sins will be punished at once or all your good works rewarded at once for all of eternity and there will be no amelioration without the intercession of an angel or a saint. Shortly after Paddy died, she asked the new curate what the next life looked like, almost in desperation, because the young fellow wasn't practised in his ministry and seemed to be reaching for things to say to her. He was sitting at the table drinking tea and he seemed shy and she thought he might even be about to cry. She nearly asked him how he'd gotten himself roped into this situation. Was he the youngest son of a big farmer or the one least likely to enter a profession? Was that still the way it worked? Surely not. She heard the diocese was desperate and boys like the one before her were pure gold dust to them. And the gold dust seemed relieved to have been asked a question with such an obvious answer. Well, Mrs Gladney, he'd begun, and she'd told him there to call her Kit, and he'd reddened and paused and then continued, Well, Kit, what's beyond this life, for faithful people, is an eternity in the company of Christ our saviour. And he smiled across at her and she'd thought that he was quite a nice-looking boy and she'd forgotten herself for a moment and said, Feck it. Eternity is a long time. I wonder is He any bit of craic?

But she thinks a lot about eternity, these days, and why

wouldn't she? Isn't it the dwelling place now of most of the people she's truly loved? She has an idea about how it works. How time never really passes. All things and all happenings are one, and their arrangement along a line dictated by the ticking of a clock is just a story man made up for himself. A way not to be overwhelmed by the idea of for ever, of not existing for ever, of not having existed for some previous for ever. And so these little bits of things she sees, these visions she attributes to Paddy's continued presence, are in a way a sense she gets of other moments in the same time, of some spreading outwards of the truth of things from a central point that she supposes to be God. And Paddy brings her closer to His whispered voice. She knew the falseness of that old priest's threats and the accidental truth at the heart of what the younger priest in his kindness and embarrassment had said. And she knew the love of God, because she could feel it the very same way she felt Paddy's love for her, all the days of their life together, and she feels it still.

Send him home to me, Paddy, she whispers, as she always does at the end of her prayers, and she raises the cross of her beads to her lips. As she lowers her hands she hears from the boreen the clang of the latch of the middle gate. She stands and sees through the window a tall black man in shirtsleeves walking towards the garden gate and she feels for a tiny part of a moment a thrill in her heart at the sight of lovely Alexander, home from his day's work. As she remembers it can't be Alexander, she sees, following the man, a girl with her hair tightly braided who could only be the man's daughter because she has the same sharp cheekbones and smiling eyes, and alongside the girl, pointing upwards towards the cottage, a young man with a scrubby beard and hair too long to be decent, and she says

227

aloud, to herself, to the house, to the spirit of her husband and all the people of this land, of this green hillside, this place of lambs and calves and deep, rich earth, Thanks be to God. There he is now. Thanks be to God. And she crosses the kitchen towards the cottage door, untying her apron as she goes.

Acknowledgements

Thanks:

To you, Reader, for allowing me to be a writer; to the booksellers who keep us all alive; to Fiona Murphy, Editorial Director at Transworld Ireland, and Brian Langan, my editor, for your friendship and support, and for saving this book with your cool heads and unerring eyes; to Larry Finlay, Bill Scott-Kerr, Alison Barrow, Kathryn Court, Victoria Savanh, Kate Samano, Hazel Orme, Alice Youell, Fíodhna Ní Ghríofa, Helen Edwards, Antonia Whitton and everyone at Doubleday Ireland, Penguin Random House Ireland, Transworld UK, and Penguin US; to Antony Farrell, Daniel Caffrey, Ruth Hallinan and everyone at The Lilliput Press; to Marianne Gunn O'Connor; to Owen Gent; to Sarah Moore-Fitzgerald, Joseph O'Connor, Martin Dyar, Gavin McCrea, Rob Doyle, and all of my colleagues, students and friends at the University of Limerick; to my dear Mary, Daniel, John, Lindsey, Aoibhinn, Christopher and Katie; to my mother, Anne Ryan, who holds everything together for all of us; to my father, Donie Ryan, whose love

I still feel and whose beautiful voice I still hear every day; to Thomas and Lucy, who bring me constant joy; and to Anne Marie, who saves me, over and over again.

Donal Ryan is from Nenagh in County Tipperary. His first three novels, *The Spinning Heart*, *The Thing About December* and *All We Shall Know*, and his short-story collection *A Slanting of the Sun*, have all been published to major acclaim. *The Spinning Heart* won the *Guardian* First Book Award, the EU Prize for Literature (Ireland), and Book of the Year at the Irish Book Awards; it was shortlisted for the International IMPAC Dublin Literary Award, longlisted for the Man Booker Prize and the Desmond Elliott Prize, and was voted 'Irish Book of the Decade'. His fourth novel, *From a Low and Quiet Sea*, was longlisted for the Man Booker Prize and shortlisted for the Costa Novel Award 2018.

A former civil servant, Donal lectures in Creative Writing at the University of Limerick. He lives with his wife Anne Marie and their two children just outside Limerick City.